THE IMPUDENT ONES

Also by Marguerite Duras

THE
IMPUDENT ONES

A NOVEL

MARGUERITE DURAS

TRANSLATED FROM THE FRENCH BY
KELSEY L. HASKETT

THE
NEW
PRESS

NEW YORK
LONDON

© Editions GALLIMARD, Paris, 1992
English translation © 2021 The New Press
"The Story Behind *The Impudent Ones*" © 2021 Jean Vallier

Originally published in France as *Les impudents* by Editions Gallimard, 1992
Published in the United States by The New Press, New York, 2021
Distributed by Two Rivers Distribution

ISBN 978-1-62097-651-7 (hc)
ISBN 978-1-62097-660-9 (ebook)
CIP data is available

This work received support from the French Ministry of Foreign Affairs and
the Cultural Services of the French Embassy in the United States through their
publishing assistance program.

The New Press publishes books that promote and enrich public discussion and
understanding of the issues vital to our democracy and to a more equitable world.
These books are made possible by the enthusiasm of our readers; the support of a
committed group of donors, large and small; the collaboration of our many partners in
the independent media and the not-for-profit sector; booksellers, who often hand-sell
New Press books; librarians; and above all by our authors.

www.thenewpress.com

Book design and composition by Bookbright Media
This book was set in Bembo

Printed in the United States of America

2 4 6 8 10 9 7 5 3 1

To my brother,
Jacques D.,
whom I never knew

CONTENTS

TRANSLATOR'S NOTE

This note is intended to provide additional clarity to the family relationships described in the novel, as well as to its setting. The Grant-Taneran family is composed first of all of Mrs. Grant-Taneran, previously a widow with the married name of Grant, who brought two children into her second marriage, Jacques Grant and Maud Grant. When Mrs. Grant married Mr. Taneran, they had another son, Henry Taneran. All together they constitute the Grant-Taneran family, more frequently known as the Taneran family. As well, Mrs. Grant-Taneran is often referred to simply as Mrs. Taneran, and her first two children simply as Maud or Jacques Grant.

The novel begins in the family's apartment in the Parisian suburb of Clamart, with Maud looking out the window toward another Parisian suburb named Sèvres. The story soon moves to the area around Uderan, the family estate situated in southwest France, and returns near the end to Clamart. One final change in location takes place, to complete the novel.

THE IMPUDENT ONES

PART I

CHAPTER 1

MAUD OPENED THE WINDOW AND THE DISTANT SOUNDS OF
the valley filled the room. The sun was setting. It left in its
wake massive clouds that clustered together and rushed blindly toward a chasm of light. The seventh floor, where they
were living, seemed breathtakingly high. The view around
them revealed a deep and resonant landscape that stretched
right out to the somber streak of the hills of Sèvres. Between
this distant horizon crammed with factories and suburbs and
the apartment high in the open sky, the air, brimming with a
fine mist, appeared thick and murky, like water.

Maud stayed by the window for a minute, her arms stretched
out on the balcony railing and her head tilted to the side in
the pose of an idle child. But her face was pale and etched
with boredom. When she turned back toward the bedroom
and closed the window, the humming of the valley suddenly
stopped, as if she had closed the sluice gate of a river.

At the far end of the dining room stood the buffet. It was
a very ordinary piece of furniture from the period of Henry

II, but with time it had taken on the role of a silent character in the Grant-Taneran home. It had followed the family and they had eaten their meals off its chipped dishes for more than twenty years. Its style and the disorder that reigned in its shelves revealed a strange absence of taste. It was obvious to anyone who saw the buffet that the Grant-Tanerans never chose or bought furniture but made do with average-looking, more or less suitable pieces of furniture that had haphazardly been passed down to them through various inheritances.

Thus it was that they gathered around the Henry II–style buffet on the evenings they arrived home from their trips. And those evenings were always the most trying because they realized that they hadn't yet left each other and that their old sideboard continued to observe them like the image of their despair.

Tonight on the buffet, the statement addressed to Jacques Grant from the Tavares Bank lay waiting for someone to open it. These statements regarding his debts often came at a bad time. This was an especially bad day because Jacques had just lost his wife, Muriel. She had died that very day following a car accident. Jacques was weeping in his bedroom, abandoned by his family, for it concerned Muriel, whom they knew very little, and each one possessed, besides their personal reasons for not reaching out to him, a reason common to all the Grant-Tanerans, a kind of contemptuous mistrust with regard to his expression of pain. So Maud didn't go in to see Jacques, even with the excuse of the statement from the bank. Moreover, it seemed to her that the statement's arrival wasn't entirely bad timing; it bitterly highlighted the fateful character of this tragic and lethargic day.

In the dining room, things like her brother's overcoat, scarf, and hat lay around in disorder, thrown over chairs. These finer objects always surprised Maud, because they were so different from her own things.

From the dining room doorway and down the dark, bare hallway came the sound of Jacques's sobbing. Maud listened attentively, her tall frame leaning against the window and her face alert. She was attractive in this pose and her beauty emanated from her face like untamed shadows. Her pale, overly wide forehead made her gray eyes look even darker. Her face, with its skin stretched out over her prominent cheekbones, was attentively immobile.

Maud felt nothing except her heart, which was beating heavily. An irresistible disgust churned inside her, but her body held it in well, like the solid banks of a torrential stream. She listened to her brother's sobs, this elder brother who at forty was twenty years her senior, weeping like a child. He had married Muriel barely a year ago, and this marriage constituted the most important event of his life, for he had never accomplished anything else. Since attaining his majority twenty years ago, he claimed jokingly that he had been content to put up with his family.

Mrs. Grant-Taneran readily accepted the idle and dangerous life her son led but, on the other hand, had never forgiven him for marrying a woman from the world he frequented. Although their quarrels were once quickly resolved, with Mrs. Taneran revealing her influence over him each time by calming down almost magically in the face of her son's growing indignation, this was no longer the case.

Maud sensed their mother's presence, alone, in the depths

of the apartment, entrenched in the kitchen, her last place of refuge. There was no sound coming from the kitchen, but Maud knew the noise of the sobbing cut through Mrs. Taneran's apparent silence. And considering the time this ordeal had lasted, since three o'clock in the afternoon (and it was already eight o'clock in the evening), the devastating effects of the sobbing must have been considerable.

The doorbell rang. The young woman went to open it. Her half brother, Henry, poked his head in with a childlike movement, barely showing his angular face and brown hair and looking like the spitting image of his father, Mr. Taneran. From Maud's low voice and the uncustomary calm that reigned, he guessed what was happening. "So it's over? Leave them alone and come with me. Let's get out of here." Maud refused. She turned on a small lamp beside her and waited.

Shortly afterward, with the sound of a grating key, Mr. Taneran emerged from the shadows of the apartment hallway. He had a short mustache, a bit charred-looking, with despondent eyes set in a face carved with wrinkles as pronounced as scars. He was thin and rather stooped.

At one time Taneran had had a respectable career teaching natural sciences at the high school in Auch. Upon retirement, he had married Mrs. Grant, who was living in the city where her first husband had worked as a tax collector.

Taneran was just returning from the Ministry of Education, where, at over sixty years of age, he had been obliged to take up work again in order to meet the heavy demands that, since his marriage, had completely absorbed his personal fortune.

In reality, his family had easily adapted to his sacrifice. It should be added that since he had started working again, Taneran had managed to escape a little from the tyranny of his family and felt quite pleased about it. He had never become used to the inevitable constraints of family life and lived, moreover, in constant fear of his stepson, Jacques Grant. If he had not hesitated to marry Mrs. Grant even though she already had two children, it was because he had assumed that the older one would soon be getting along on his own.

He and Mrs. Taneran had had another son, Henry, for whom he felt a great deal of concealed tenderness, although Taneran quickly had to get used to the idea that his feelings were not at all reciprocated. Thus, to all appearances, Taneran lived a very solitary life.

On entering the apartment, he, too, understood that something unusual was going on and approached his stepdaughter in the hope that she would fill him in. "If you want, I'll serve you dinner right away," was all Maud felt like saying. At that moment, Mrs. Taneran called out in a weak, husky voice, "Maud, serve dinner to your father—it's ready."

The young woman hurried to unroll a wax tablecloth, set a place, and enter the kitchen. Her mother had finally turned on the light and was reading the newspaper. Without raising her head, Mrs. Taneran repeated in a gloomy tone, "Everything's ready. You can eat with your father, and if your brother Henry comes back, you can serve him, too." Maud did not acknowledge that her brother certainly would not come home that night.

Dinner was quick. Taneran wanted nothing more than to retire to his room. Nevertheless, he asked Maud in a low voice, "She's dead, isn't she?" Maud nodded, and he added, "Fundamentally, you know, I don't feel any ill will toward him. It's very unfortunate." He was masticating his food, and in the silence of the apartment it made a bizarre, irritating noise. Before going out he turned and said, "I don't want to disturb your mother. Please say good night to her for me."

His bedroom and the dining room shared an adjoining wall. Maud could hear him walking in his room for a long time. Under his feet the bare floor made a gentle creaking and cracking noise.

Maud felt at peace. For too long trouble had been brewing, that is, ever since Jacques and his wife had begun to be short of money.

As far back as she could remember, Jacques had been in financial difficulty, except for the first few months of his marriage. He was always in need of cash. This was by far the most important thing in his life. He existed in the center of a whirlwind, his head spinning over money.

Whenever he had any, he became another man. He possessed such an acute sense of his own inanity that he spent recklessly, throwing money out the window, deluding himself by using up funds in a few days that could have lasted a month. He smartened up his wardrobe, invited all his friends, and, with the magnificent disdain that his temporary opulence allowed him, didn't appear at home for a whole week, avoiding this family who knew how to stretch out money so shamefully, so miserably, like others who hold back on using their full strength or enjoying pleasure, or like a dutiful servant who spares his masters any grief.

When he no longer had anything left but a few bills and some change in his pant pockets, he bitterly measured his slim possibilities. He would set out on the hunt, trying to pawn off a friend's old jalopy, and, not succeeding, would turn to gambling, going flat broke right away. Finally, worn-out and unapproachable, he would put himself into the hands of the members of the gang that had followed the same leads as he had for years and knew all the rackets. (Perhaps they were the only ones who felt any sympathy for him, although he detested them because they had seen him in the most shameful moments of his life.)

His wife's money had disappeared as fast as the profits from his shady affairs. For several months, the couple had led what one would call a futile life, because it made no sense, but which, in reality, is very difficult to live: an idle and perfectly egotistical life, even though it appears generous, which consists of an uninterrupted series of moments of pleasure and respite, a continuous exorcism of boredom.

Muriel, who had entrusted her fortune to her husband, always remained ignorant of the ways in which he used it. She "detested expense accounts and never bothered with them." Jacques was soon rushing around like a madman, trying to cover expenses he had allowed himself to incur.

Soon he began to beg. The little his family could give him had become appreciable of late. "I know you can't give me much, but do what you can. A hundred-franc bill will be enough. I just need to hang on."

"I thought your wife was rich," countered his mother. "Don't you think I have enough expenses already?"

He didn't answer so as not to spoil things, guessing that

his difficulties were on the rise. And indeed, Mrs. Taneran had let go of less and less money, at the same time that her son's needs continued to grow. This money, obtained through promises and pleas, represented more and more of the essentials for Muriel: stockings ("she has nothing left to wear"), the rent, or money needed to redeem a piece of jewelry, part of her "family heirlooms," from the pawn shop. In the end, he stopped coming up with reasons to justify his demands. They had to eat. And again, he found appealing ways of making his requests. "She's a wonderful cook, poor dear. If only you could taste her cooking. You'll come, won't you, Mother, when we have a bit more money?"

"What about me? Don't I know how to cook? You're saying you didn't like my cooking? Go on, say so . . ." Mrs. Taneran detested him because love contains the dregs of hatred. In the end, she wasn't unhappy with his romantic misfortune.

It didn't take long for him to start playing highly emotional scenes. Stretched out as if he were sick, he would wait for someone to come and ask him what was wrong. "Nothing— it's nothing. But I won't go back home tonight without a thing. She's no doubt waiting for me, but I prefer not to see her again, to disappear." The gang he had left a few months earlier had let him down. And so, acting on a supreme sense of family solidarity, his sister, brother, and stepfather all dug down to the bottom of their purses or pockets—all of them— Maud, Henry, and even Taneran. They gave him, secretly, twenty, thirty, or fifty francs, with a feverish joy. He took pleasure, however, in vexing them. "Mother went along with it?"

"No, she doesn't want to hear any more about it."

Unshakeable as well as astute, Mrs. Taneran had thus guided her ship and governed her son's destiny. Soon loathing his own home with Muriel, he had come back for dinner more and more often. His mother never gave him too much money at once, so that he didn't have the impression he could control her, but always just enough for him to have the essentials and so that he would return.

Suddenly, however, he disappeared for a couple of weeks. They thought he had succeeded in some business deal. And it was shortly afterward that the saga of the mail with the letterhead from the Tavares Bank had begun. The letters came regularly, every four weeks. Although leaving him indifferent in the beginning, while he still had money, they soon threw him into a terrible state.

Someone who has never experienced the feeling of being at the mercy of creditors cannot imagine the deadly aversion these greedy people inspired in him. The whole family suffered with Jacques when they saw the statements arriving from the Tavares Bank. Normally Jacques received his mail at his wife's place, but this mail he had addressed to his mother's. "Have a look on the buffet. There's a letter for you. I think it's the request for payment from Tavares."

He would bury it in his pocket, crumpling it and seemingly digesting the piece of paper for an hour, literally. He sank into sickening daydreams in which it was easy to guess that Tavares himself had become the victim of a massacre. And then, for a certain time, he stopped coming to get his letters, believing he had thus done away with their existence. But he quickly found himself so destitute that he had to accept coming back.

Right away his mother cornered him. "Can't you tell me what you've done, Jacques? After your father's death I had to borrow, and I know how tough it is." The only thing he had deigned to reply was, "It's a debt with short but frequent due dates; in my situation I could never have paid a big amount all at once."

"Why all this secrecy? Why not tell your wife?" Mrs. Taneran would have liked her daughter-in-law to suffer in turn from the agony of being in debt. But Jacques had not involved his wife in any questions regarding money, and for good reason. By the same token, he had never wanted her to know his family, because it repulsed him. She had died without visiting even once.

No doubt Jacques had loved her more than any other, and in a more sincere and lasting way. For a long time Muriel had kept up the image of the ideal woman that she had had at the beginning of their relationship.

The tragedy had erupted this particular night, brutal and unexpected. It was probably going to resolve the tangled mess they were trapped in and strangely facilitate its elimination. In reality, each one had expected this conclusion throughout the months that Jacques and his mother's ordeal had lasted.

Toward ten o'clock in the evening, Maud heard her older brother calling her. As she approached, Jacques lifted his swollen face and then sank back into his pillow, finding himself there, as it were, at the heart of his sadness. His suffering absorbed him as much as it prostrated him. He was no doubt amazed that it was possible to go on living with this sorrow.

She sat down beside him and partially opened up his tense fingers, grabbing a strand of hair that he was clenching. Immediately he slumped down, let himself go slack, and moaned in total abandonment. "No doubt about it, she was a true blonde," said Maud. "Her hair was smooth and fine, like a child's." He gave a weak, almost complicit smile, to show her she had fully grasped the direction of his thoughts. He cast off his pain for a moment and smiled at the memory of Muriel.

Maud explained to him at length that he shouldn't consider this death to be an unusual event. What was extraordinary was that, as she spoke to him, an inner voice repeated her own words, which took on a different meaning than the one she wanted to give them. As for Jacques, he wished only to bring back the memory of the deceased. He described that horrible night when she had been brought to him with her chest crushed.

"The chums who were with her brought her back to me," he said. "They left her with me because they thought she had had it. But even though she had lost consciousness, she was still breathing, and I kept her all night before taking her to the hospital."

He stopped from time to time and then resumed, looking absorbed in his thoughts. "She didn't have any wounds, so I thought she had passed out. I put her under the covers, but little by little she got cold and I felt the warmth of her body leaving her. I thought at a certain point I was going crazy. She was laughing, I swear, the same way as when she made fun of me. I began to talk to her idiotically all night . . . It was only at daybreak that I understood, when I looked at her in the light. I saw the grimace I had taken for her smile. I took her to the hospital—she didn't die until this evening."

"What do you think . . . ?" Maud asked.

"I have no idea, none. She told me she had never been so happy. But there's no reason to think it was an accident. The street was free of traffic and it wasn't raining. Even the chums are in doubt. I never caused her the slightest bit of pain, though. She was the only one, the only one I ever loved."

He readily repeated the last sentence. As soon as he shook himself and stopped being absorbed in a very private contemplation of his sorrow, he began to cry again. "The only one," he kept repeating, "the only one I ever loved."

Being embarrassed, he didn't know quite how to express himself. "I called you because I don't have a cent . . . I had to borrow so I could have her better taken care of. And you know I can't ask Mother for that . . ." Maud looked at him with his big, lucid eyes, his face devoid of all expression. She thought about the letter from the bank that was waiting on the buffet.

They had already given him so much money! Didn't he always skillfully extract some benefit from the emotions he caused? In the past minute he had been playing up his misfortune to his advantage. She hesitated, however, to leave the room. It was astonishing to see him lower himself to this point, just to get a bit of cash. And, of course, she might be mistaken. Jacques himself, who seemed so pitiful, probably remained convinced of his own sincerity.

Finding her composure again, she weighed the pros and cons quickly, like someone who is used to these kinds of deals. Already, Jacques's look had hardened because she had been slow to reply. "How much do you want?"

He specified the amount in a small, humble voice. He felt obliged to add, his eyes glistening as much from crying as from greed, "I rushed around all day trying to hunt down some dough, but there was no way to get hold of any of my buddies. It's ridiculous, for an amount like that, ridiculous."

Maud didn't answer. She got her purse, counted the little money she had, and replied, "You'll have the rest tomorrow." Embarrassed, she avoided looking at him. She didn't hand him the bills, but just put them on his chest.

CHAPTER 2

JACQUES BURIED HIS WIFE THE NEXT DAY. MRS. TANERAN accompanied him. They felt suddenly reconciled upon returning from this bleak ceremony. In the coolness of the morning, the sap made the buds burst open, and puffs of air already carried the odor of hot tarmac and dust. The smell made one's nose tingle and put winter far behind. Summer was coming, early. Jacques and his mother talked about leaving for Uderan.

"That will put you back on your feet, dear, and at the same time I can keep a closer watch on my own interests. Besides, we haven't gone for such a long time . . ."

Jacques didn't say anything. He already felt his strength returning. Since his childhood illnesses, he had never again appreciated the comfort of convalescence and almost dreaded the moment when his insatiable nature would take over. For now, he let himself glide happily down the gentle slope of the sunny boulevard he was descending on his mother's arm. He should have been sad, but he wasn't really, although he didn't mind being consoled, while his stiff bearing and toneless, dreary voice expressed a decency he felt proper to keep for some time to come. Because he remained quiet, his mother added, "As for Taneran, he'll get along fine without us, since obviously he won't want to come, as usual." (When she mentioned her husband to her older son, she always called him "Taneran.")

Uderan was in Dordogne. The Tanerans had settled there after their marriage. Henry was born there. Although the purchase of the property had soon proved to be a poor investment for them, they had nevertheless lived there for seven years and had never thought of selling it. When they had gone to live in Paris, despite the low income derived from the tenant farmers, they had kept the place.

Mrs. Taneran remained the only one who occasionally remembered its existence, whenever she feared the future darkened by political events. "Happily we have Uderan! Blessed are those who possess land!" she would proclaim sententiously. They had lived through some long, difficult years confined to a few rooms of the house, which was too big.

For seven years they devoted themselves to restoring the estate. But Uderan had belonged to a whole series of people who, not coming from the region, understood very little about how to cultivate it, and it was extremely dilapidated. The fruit trees, poorly pruned over a long period of time, and the vines, much too old, produced less and less fruit. Only the fields had not suffered too much, as they fed the six cows of the tenant farmer, whereas the woods that encircled the domain, which people had neglected to cut for years, were quite dense.

Mrs. Taneran was soon discouraged, and overnight her enthusiasm for the task vanished. She suddenly got rid of things, like people, after having fiercely loved them, unable to remain deeply attached to the same thing. Her fervor, which generally ended up overcoming all resistance, failed when she attacked Uderan. All her attempts were in vain. The farmers laughed at her desperate efforts, and she left, leaving the property to Dedde, the tenant farmer. This caretaker managed to live off the land, but Mrs. Taneran never received any ground rent and considered herself fortunate that Uderan didn't cost her anything.

If, this May morning, she was suddenly seized by the desire to return, it was because she felt the need to get over this sad story. For the Grant-Tanerans, Uderan represented, in fact, a kind of high place whose memory haunted them. They believed they had lived and suffered there in a state of hardship but could not look back without a sense of loss at their life there, before living a sad existence in Paris, in which each one was merely the witness of the weaknesses and failures of the others.

When Mrs. Taneran suggested to her son that they leave for Uderan, he did not reply, and she understood that he approved. It was rare that she had him in the palm of her hand like this, attentive to her words, both submissive and charmed. Didn't he usually flee the house as soon as he woke up? The only thing that brought the Grant-Tanerans together was the table they shared twice a day, around which they continued to detest one another and devour their food while keeping a close eye on one another . . . However, the presence of her son did not fill this mother with happiness, for she could not bring herself to forget the poor girl they had just buried. Even though Mrs. Taneran was in no way responsible for this misfortune, she couldn't manage to remain calm.

From time to time she looked at her son, who was tall and handsome, with disconcertingly good looks for a man. What hadn't she hoped for as a result of her son's attractiveness? She rediscovered in him the exalted hope that had lifted her spirits when he was born. But after she'd been let down the first time, her other pregnancies, much later, had been less glorious than this one.

Jacques was now forty . . . She always agreed to his whims, and he always came back to her after each experience, each youthful indiscretion. Her lot in life was to receive him when he felt like running to her, and she never asked for anything but to take care of him like a rich bourgeois. If she tried to give him advice concerning his future, he shot back with his usual fierceness, threatening to leave. Now he was reaching maturity and she was witnessing his decline . . . And she found herself to be so much at fault when it came to her son that she, too, preferred not to think about it much. Why, for example, hadn't she been able to warn him about the dangerous game that had brought him to this risky affair, whose outcome could have been disastrous, for she wasn't sure, in the end, that Muriel hadn't been killed.

Mrs. Taneran went over the tragedy in her mind, her thoughts naturally coming back to her daughter, Maud, this young woman who was still hers. Wasn't it Maud who had given the money to her brother? She should have found out how Maud had gotten it, but every step was painful when it came to Maud, and she preferred admitting that she was incapable of being heard by any of her children. Without her, however, the family would not have existed; each one would have fled the others for good, she was sure. Mother of this grown son, of this decidedly mean and ungrateful daughter, of this perverse young man, and wife of this man who didn't leave on account of her good cooking, she believed, and because he had succeeded in constructing a bastion of indifference on this unstable ground, she owed herself to everyone. For an instant she wished she were a peaceful old woman whose job was over and for whom it would be easy to die or live the way she wanted. She had been dreaming of a quiet life for some time. Why did she keep her children around her, especially her oldest son? Why did she keep him so closely under her supervision? Why did she accustom him to not being able to do without her presence, abnormally prolonging her maternal role? Yes, she should have separated herself from Jacques as quickly as possible. Sometimes this thought crossed her mind like lightning and filled her with fear . . . One should be careful of children who plunder everything one has . . . It seemed now that she could no longer even imagine the end of this servitude.

Weariness fell upon her, brutally. The sunny boulevard continued to invite her to taste the joy of a morning in May, yet she suddenly felt deflated. "Let's take a taxi," she exclaimed.

But as soon as they were settled in the car, as soon as her son looked at her with a surprised and disapproving look, she sank submissively back into her role.

CHAPTER 3

MAUD OFTEN THOUGHT ABOUT NO LONGER COMING HOME.
However, each evening brought her back. Her attitude might
have seemed strange, but it was also that of her brothers and
stepfather, who, in spite of themselves, never failed to reappear
every evening, just as they had for such a long time! Had they
been transported to the ends of the earth, they would have
come back one day or another, feeling the strong pull of the
family circle, where nothing, not even idleness, could lessen
the interest they had for one another. In reality, no matter
how much they repeated that they were going to leave, none
of them really thought about it seriously.

As seldom as they occurred, there were still some good
times to be had at the Grant-Tanerans'. Peace settled in on
its own, like a lull. The strange antagonism between them
would have been more striking had it not alternated with
times of respite during which they caught their breath.

Immediately after dinner, the family scattered. Taneran
stayed in his room, where he savored his only moments of

true happiness. Elsewhere, even in a quiet hotel room where he would have been just as alone, he would have been bored, for he needed to hear the indistinct sounds his family made: Maud giving little coughs on the other side of the wall as she waited for her brothers to leave . . . his wife, moving about randomly, coming and going with impulsive steps, creating an atmosphere of childish insensibility around her . . . Taneran had loved her for a long time and still loved her. Since the time of their stay at Uderan, he had hoped that one evening she would reappear and talk to him gently, but since they had stopped sharing a room, she no longer came. Even though she was old and worn-out, having never taken things easy, Taneran kept waiting for her and could not get rid of the hope that one day she would leave her work aside and come . . .

Taneran listened for the departure of the two brothers.

Jacques Grant's voice humiliated Taneran and would have made him leap out of his room if he had had the courage. (He was lying when he said that his stepson left him indifferent.) As soon as Jacques left, Taneran asked Henry, in an overly attentive tone that should have flattered him, "Which way are you heading?" The younger son rarely agreed to leave with his older brother. It was another small satisfaction for the father, who nevertheless knew that this son would soon leave, closing the door behind him with the finesse of a cat. For two years, Henry had also gone out and run around in the evenings . . .

Sometimes, before going out, Henry would knock at his father's door and Maud knew what he was up to. One had to be scraping the bottom of the barrel, after having been refused by the mother, to ask for money from Taneran. ("Go ask your father, that old cheapskate!") Taneran, however, was glad to have someone turn to him for help. Foreseeing, though, the danger he would be in if he revealed to his son how anxious he was to help him, he showed none of his pleasure. When his son ran down the stairs four at a time, Taneran naïvely believed that it was the joy of having four hundred francs in his pocket that excited the young man.

When someone said of one of the sons, "He's with Taneran; he's asking something of Taneran," everyone was aware of the fact that a silent drama was being played out, worse than a violent scene, because Taneran was in no way an opponent and nothing more could add to his denigration. The only thing that could bring the Grant-Taneran children down in their own eyes was this final step toward their victim. Only the lack of money could justify it.

Maud could hardly stand these scenes, which nevertheless repeated themselves fairly frequently. Still young, she took part in everyone's life, suffering for Henry and unable to watch Jacques's misfortune with passivity. Thus, when her mother worried, at dawn, at not seeing one or the other of her sons come home, the young woman got up and trembled with the same fear.

When Henry left, in turn, the second clacking of the door left the apartment in a silence that Mrs. Taneran's noisy activity soon dissipated. Maud remained alone, lost in thought in the small sitting room.

At her age, each season brought something new. Thus, for more than a year, Henry hadn't taken her with him when he went out, and an uneasiness reigned between them, inexplicable to her. Moreover, since the passing of her sister-in-law, they all fled one another, and she herself was not looking for company. It seemed that for a long time they had waited for an event that would put an end to the ascendancy Jacques exercised over the family. They were disappointed. Jacques began going out again and taking back the upper hand he had in the household, from which the death of his wife had momentarily exempted him. Since this event, on the other hand, he had become more and more difficult, hardly being able to stand the presence of Taneran at the table. Even if Jacques went out as much as before, he did not want it to be said that he suffered less for his loss, which is why he feigned an exasperation intended to simulate sorrow.

One would have said that he felt responsible for the family and that the charge he took on gave him exorbitant rights. Mrs. Taneran helped him maintain this belief, moreover, in order to keep him close to her. "You are the oldest one," she would repeat to him. "If I die, you will have to marry off your sister and take care of Henry. I can't count on Taneran. You understand the younger ones well and will know how to keep them in check, I know." If Jacques had not felt useful to his family, perhaps he would not have stood the total inanity of the existence he had led for twenty years.

From time to time, Taneran ventured out of his room after the young men had gone out. The upcoming departure for Uderan now gave him the pretext to talk with his wife of their interests, and he found it pleasant that Mrs. Taneran came to join him every evening in the small sitting room.

The two women let Taneran talk as much as he wanted to, with a voice that ended up tiring them, precisely because it never got past its unhealthy nervousness.

Knowing the topic to be dear to his wife, he once again

repeated that "Jacques should take up residence at Uderan instead of hanging around miserably in Paris." But, unfortunately, one can dream about something for a long time and be disappointed when the opportunity arises for it to be realized, because it's always less dazzling than one's hopes. Mrs. Taneran hesitated to suggest that her son take on their property, because she had hoped for a long time that he would come back to it himself, at some point in his life.

But once again her adventurous spirit took over; to convince him to settle down it would be necessary to confront his horribly bad temper. Now, Mrs. Taneran both adored and feared her older son. So she preferred not to listen to her husband.

But he, counting on her silence, insisted even more! "After, it will be too late for him. And as for the others, don't even talk about them! You realize yourself, my dear Marie, that since our son quit school, he hasn't done anything. If we don't stop him in time, he'll follow the same path as his older brother. And I think that for Maud it's just as bad, as you well know . . ."

Taneran believed he could soften the harshness of his words by coating his sentences with verbal varnish. For a long time, moreover, he had spoken like that to confound his step-children, who spoke with great vulgarity, precisely because they detested him. It was also, however, because Maud and Henry had gotten used to Jacques's vocabulary, which was forever changing and picking up new expressions, depending on the people with whom he rubbed shoulders. Thus, since knowing his wife, and even though she had died, Jacques affected a form of scornful, feminine refinement in his talk.

As soon as she was brought into the conversation, Maud

laughed sarcastically, partly closing her eyes and shrugging her shoulders, her head tilted back with a look of unsparing mockery, already taking unconscious womanly pleasure in confusing a man by the inconsistency of her mystery.

"You can laugh!" he retorted. "Who wouldn't be worried at seeing you act with such freedom? Only this family could show such indifference toward a child."

Mrs. Taneran got upset. She planned to raise her daughter the way she wanted to. Hadn't she done that with Henry and avoided the worst with a child like Jacques? "Enough with the girl! As for Jacques, I'll see when we get there. I won't leave him at Uderan if he's going to be bored. After what's happened, let's be careful. We have to watch out for the worst."

The worst was sometimes insignificant, sometimes terrifying, depending on whether it was brought up in distress or in relative calm. It appeared sometimes in the everyday flow of existence, having the well-defined and always discouraging appearance of a crime, a suicide, an important theft. It existed outside the home, like an epidemic that prowls around the city but has not yet touched you. And they were glad to settle for avoiding the worst in life . . .

"What could happen to him at Uderan, even if he's bored, Mother?"

The mother stared at the night, considering the omens. "You're still too young—keep quiet."

Mrs. Taneran preferred not to put anything into words, troubled by that superstitious fear that adds to the emotions something like a halo of darkness. Taneran, vexed, with his head as low and withered as that of a dead man propped up in a sitting position, stayed quiet in his armchair. So his wife offered him a cup of herbal tea by way of consolation. It reminded them—especially Maud—of many things. When she was little, at Uderan, her brothers took on this task when Taneran had a cold. Mrs. Taneran had to be very angry with her husband to refuse him this small token of happiness, which is something one would do for anyone, even for the first person to come along. Maud was always afraid to walk through the house. Often the cup arrived half-empty in the overflowing saucer, but Taneran would pour it back into the cup and drink it while noisily breathing in. Maud, sitting on a stool, would wait until he was done. While drinking, he would ask himself questions that made him so unhappy that his voice wept.

"I wonder what we came to do here on this woeful property. I was unhappy at that awful school when we lived in Auch, but at least there I was respected, whereas here . . ." At that time, his wife was no longer concerned about him, totally absorbed by the work of the farm and focused on her children.

He questioned Maud, to keep her near him, in a cutting, complicit tone of voice. "You were afraid to come to Uderan, weren't you? Do you like it here?"

Yes, Maud liked it. The proof that Taneran wasn't one of them was that he didn't like it. For her, their stay at Uderan had no beginning and seemingly no end. As for Auch, she could hardly remember it.

"What are they up to in the kitchen? Tell them they disgust me, do you hear?" She refused to answer Taneran. He finally gave her his cup; she ran as fast as she could to the kitchen door, where her fear vanished. She would then sit near Henry by the fire, silently.

She liked Taneran in this way, just as one becomes attached

to certain inanimate objects because they remind one of certain things and prevent the past from entirely disappearing. The terror she used to feel in the hallways of Uderan was reflected in Taneran's bleary, lost eyes, when she thought back on it. Her first dislike of someone went back to those evenings; it had the smell of lime-blossom tea blended with the sound of his breathing. The words that she alone knew him to say—"What are they up to in the kitchen? Tell them they disgust me"—contained a rare poison: the cowardliness of a man and his misery.

When by chance Jacques came home earlier than usual, before the three accomplices had gone to bed, he was indignant. Jacques Grant had no idea, in fact, that his mother chatted in the evening with her husband and daughter. Because he came home earlier since the death of his wife, he became exasperated, and even more so because he suspected they spoke more freely in that small circle than with him.

He cracked open the door into the sitting room, wearing a bitter smile. Nevertheless, he said calmly to Taneran, "So, you're there, are you?" Maud didn't move. A newspaper his stepson carelessly threw in landed at Taneran's feet. "Here, if you want it, it's the latest copy of *Paris-Soir*; it'll keep you busy if you're bored."

The door closed again. In the next room, you could hear someone whistling a popular tune on key. Standing up, Taneran looked at the newspaper at his feet. Before going out, he doled out an idiocy to his wife, taking advantage of the fact that she couldn't answer him back, for fear of being heard by her son. "My dear, I feel sorry for you. The impropriety of your son toward me leaves me indifferent, but for you it's a beginning; you have created your own misfortune, and you're still doing it."

Then he went into his room, haughtily and miserably. Maud, in turn, snuck into her bedroom without saying a word. She undressed in the dark, quickly and without making a sound, so that no one would recall her forgotten existence, as insignificant as a shipwreck in the middle of the sea. A kind of blind rage threw her onto the small bed, which she grabbed with both arms. But it soon passed, melting like the fear that she felt at Uderan, a fear that seemed inconceivable to her with the coming of the new day.

PART II

CHAPTER 4

THE UDERAN DOMAIN WAS LOCATED IN SOUTHWEST LOT, IN the rough and unpopulated part of Upper Quercy, on the edge of Dordogne and Lot-et-Garonne.*

The two villages of Semoic and The Pardal shared administrative and religious functions; they were both wine-growing and fruit-producing villages, one perched in the pine forests of the plateau, the other down by the water, on the Dior River. Although the domain was under the jurisdiction of the town of Semoic, at the Feast of Corpus Christi it was the priest from The Pardal who came to bless it.

Uderan occupied one of the best-situated slopes of this rugged region, and one of the highest, after the slope of Ostel. The castle of Ostel dated back to the thirteenth century. It dominated a region stretching for fifty kilometers in all directions and remained one of the most powerful seigneuries of Upper Quercy.

---

* Lot, Dordogne, and Lot-et-Garonne are departments in southwest France, that is, administrative districts similar to counties.—Trans.

Few city dwellers traveled that far for their holidays, but there were some who owned family estates in the region. It was because of the low cost of land that Taneran had been able to move there.

The vines, cultivated for centuries in this region, no longer possessed their former reputation, except in the eyes of those who proudly considered their wines to be better than all those, nonetheless famous, of neighboring regions.

The Tanerans were not able to lodge in their home, which had been abandoned for ten years and had become uninhabitable. The ceilings leaked and grass grew in between the tiles in the bedrooms. Only the wine cellar and the plum dehydrator were in good shape, being for the common use of the farmers leasing the land and the owners.

The positive observations Mrs. Taneran made were limited to the fact that the grounds themselves had not suffered too much from abandonment. The dwelling, which had had most of its furniture carried off to Paris, seemed practically beyond use.

The day of their arrival was gloomy. They had to find temporary lodging. Thus, they did not anticipate what happened next: the Tanerans were obliged to board at the Pecresse home.

The Pecresses were the neighbors closest to Uderan. Their great-grandparents had been tenant farmers on the estate and had bought the tenant farm on which they were working when one of the property owners had been obliged to leave. Since then, the property had regularly become enlarged with each property transfer the owners undertook, one by one, in order to cope with the upkeep of the large dwelling on the second tenant farm.

A beautiful landowner's home and a big garden now flanked the former tenant farm. The Pecresses, having become wealthy farmers, had not curtailed their ambitions. Unfortunately, they had only one son, and it was around him that they built their ambitions.

People had referred to him, at a certain point, as the most eligible bachelor of the region, as much for the size of the inheritance that awaited him as for his attractive bearing. On top of that, he had completed some studies, which conferred on him a certain intellectual prestige in the village.

However, John turned twenty-five without having made up his mind about marriage. He never put in an appearance anywhere, and his mother saw to it that he did not go out with anyone. He became shy and withdrawn. The young women got discouraged. In his golden solitude, John appeared inaccessible. People thought about him less. Or rather, they began to shudder at the thought of what life must be like for him and his overbearing, redheaded mother, Mrs. Pecresse, at the Old Tenant Farm, as it was called.

When his paternal grandmother died, one September evening, after a glorious day of grape harvesting, tenderness disappeared from John's life for good. He no longer had anyone but his mother for company, and he suspected that she loved him too much. With no outlet, the passion this mother felt for her son expressed itself as aggressively as if she detested him. The violent feelings of the one and the meek passivity of the other never stopped growing, although in the course of the monotonous life they lived, their sentiments never found any opportunity to manifest themselves. The atmosphere of the Old Tenant Farm became as strange as the somber classical setting of an intimate drama, whose art consists of never bringing together the only two characters representing the very substance of the drama, and whose confrontation would empty it in a single stroke of its psychological interest.

The father of the Pecresse family found happiness in his work. In relation to the other family members, he was the picture of discretion, which consisted of indifference, concern for his own peace, and inexpressible cowardice. This weakness gave the Pecresse father a certain charm, which made him the only inhabitant of the Old Tenant Farm whom people liked to meet. But at home, it expressed itself as treacherously as the worst spirit of intrigue and ended up making him flee the family. Moreover, he did not count in the eyes of his wife and son any more than if he had been feebleminded.

The Old Tenant Farm was as far from Semoic and The Pardal as Uderan itself. But unlike Uderan, no road went by, except for the main road, which turned fifty meters from there toward the village of Rayvre. There were shortcuts to get there from The Pardal, so few farmers took the Old Tenant Farm road to the village.

John must have waited for years for someone to pass by their farm. Their only neighbors, those from Uderan, had not come for a long time, and the silhouette of the pinewood rose before him, untamed. However, his mother still hoped to marry him off according to her own ideas.

John was looked on as a simpleton whom one could easily lead on, a good match for an able young woman, in short, if his mother had not been so vigilant. He was unhappy at home and worked as hard in the fields as an ordinary pieceworker. He could have had workers. But even if the Pecresse family spent their energy in hard labor, they hung on to their money. People soon said that John was stingy and a bit of a driveler.

His mother, who was not lacking in good sense, finally began to worry. John exceeded her hopes, and she wouldn't have been unhappy if he had been a little more at ease with the girls. To encourage him, she hired a young servant girl, because, all things considered, she would have preferred to see him embroiled in some low-class affair than to see him marry below himself or, indeed, be bitter toward life.

But John refused to touch the servant who slept beside his room. He refused to fall, even once, into the trap that he knew his mother had laid for him.

Three years passed. John was approaching thirty. The servant had stayed. The Pecresses led a laborious and well-to-do, although sad and monotonous, life in the presence of their only son, who seemed to give himself over to this chaste and solitary existence as fervently as if it had been a reprehensible passion.

This state of affairs lasted until one summer evening when, on the edge of the Dior River, where John often spent time, he met a stranger. Immediately he felt like the guilty man who, one fine day, after a long, exhausting journey, arrives in a village where his crime is unknown.

The young woman was cutting bulrushes with a small, brilliant machete. Two long black braids hung from her head down to the tall grass. Her dress of faded red stood out against the dark green of the river like the color burst of a piece of fruit against the foliage. She looked like the young woman of a fictional tale who might have wandered from her home at dusk, haunted by dreams. As soon as she saw the young man, the vision changed. She straightened up, arched her back, and called out to him casually, with an almost vulgar self-assurance. He couldn't see her face very well, for the shadows blurred its features, but he picked out its calm and mindlessly cheerful expression. He saw someone unafraid and used to talking to one and all, like vagabonds for whom all passersby are friends.

What John experienced for an instant was memorable. It was as if he awoke to the inordinate beauty of love.

Naturally, he answered her ineptly. The young woman, disconcerted, looked at him for a moment and then got back to work. John moved away but looked back quickly with each step, like someone afraid of being followed. He sat down on an alder stump and continued to consider her with a stupid look on his face, in which all human emotions jostled together, although not a single one of them succeeded in coming to the fore and taking over.

Both terrified and touched, he couldn't move. At a certain point, she began to sing. He couldn't believe his ears. The song seemed to flow in his veins like poison. Each musical phrase, undulating or piercing, astonished his flesh and turned it into something painfully sensitive.

Like a child waking up, he didn't really understand what was happening. The spectacle of his existence passed through his mind, incomprehensibly. He felt that he was being born to an unknown state of being. He thought of his chastity with horror. It paralyzed him and he felt himself stagger under its weight.

No one passed by. Only the train from Bordeaux shook the silence, followed by trails of smoke; the light that flashed from its doors streaked the sky with red glimmers.

The young woman moved away, with a bundle of bulrushes on her back and her small machete in her hand. She went in the direction of Semoic. John found himself alone on the bank of the Dior and stayed there until night closed in on him.

The next evening found him in the same place on the alder stump. He felt weakened by lack of sleep and hunger, having neither eaten nor slept since the day before. However, his nerves, like reins, held him back from making the sinuous approach of a man toward a woman.

As soon as she was once again singing and calmly taking the road back to Semoic, he was afraid. Maybe she would never come back. Thrown suddenly out of his dream, out of his fear, he found himself upright and desperately brutal.

He ran and caught up with her, and she recognized him and smiled. But he was unable to look at her face as he told her with a harsh, unsteady voice that she had no right to come and cut the bulrushes in his meadows on the Dior. He became indignant, but his inflamed voice burned only himself. Whoever might have seen these two silhouettes on the road—hers bent over under the bundle of reeds and his gesturing wildly with his two arms—would have taken them for master and slave. And that is what she subsequently became in his hands.

She appeared again the next day, and at the end of a week she gave herself to him at the same place where they had first seen each other, at the bend in the Dior at the edge of the alder woods.

Their love was complicated in the beginning, at least for him, by a sense of romantic fiction and disillusion. She let her family return home and she stayed in Semoic. She didn't miss her previous wanderings. She earned a good living by offering her services from farm to farm to do washing, harvesting, grape picking, and such.

Their affair lasted for three years. John cheated on his mistress whenever the occasion presented itself, in particular with his servant. He found his mistress cost him a lot of money, but he didn't think seriously of leaving her. He felt at ease in regard to many things with her. But he had waited for love too long and remained disappointed. He gained weight and turned into a half-wit.

The evening the Tanerans arrived, John felt intimidated. An event of this kind had never happened at the Pecresse home, where they never received anyone. He insisted that they dine in the dining room and not in the kitchen as they were used to doing, in the manner of true farmers. It was a lot of effort, but his mother could find nothing to say about it. As the servant girl moved about with her usual sluggishness that night, John spoke harshly to her, making her cry. He put on the hunting garb he usually wore only on Sundays.

When everything had been prepared according to his wishes, he waited for the Tanerans to come back from their walk over to Uderan. He had barely seen them in the morning. They had surprised him by their simple and natural deportment, and he had enjoyed talking with them. They were supposed to have lunch with the Deddes, their tenant farmers, and the day seemed long to John Pecresse. As it went by, his exuberance grew, without his really knowing why.

They came in one after another, the brothers first, and then Mrs. Taneran and Maud, dazzled by the light, all of them wearing, like a family look, an identical expression of fatigue and disdain on their faces. They no longer appeared as the travelers they had been in the morning, happy to arrive and cheerfully carrying their suitcases, talkative and youthful.

The Pecresses were feeling quite moved. The Tanerans made no attempt at conversation. They took their places on the chairs backed up against the dining room wall. No noises entered the room except those of the kitchen, which one could make out just below, near the stable of the previous home. They were hungry. Jacques yawned with boredom and a feeling of well-being.

Facing the chimney stood a magnificent china cabinet, with its molding and its porcelain gleaming. The immaculate table was shining with an unreal whiteness. A gentle, acidulous odor floated in the air, that of the plonk, or cheap wine, of Lot and the musty-smelling cask treated with sulfur, vaguely reminiscent of human perspiration.

A brief moment went by before Mrs. Pecresse called everyone for dinner. She came and apologized to her guests that everything wasn't ready and went back to the kitchen. The father must have been in the barn. He discreetly stayed in the background, like a servant. John did not yet dare to appear. Already each of the Pecresses had the same thought, without having shared it with one another. The Tanerans, for their part, found the place warm and pleasant, although rather far from the villages. But they had no precise thoughts in their minds.

Maud went out for a moment on the porch to watch the nightfall.

At the summit of the slope of which Uderan and the Old Tenant Farm occupied the middle, a few farms at The Pardal had feeble oil lamps that were twinkling. It was mild out; there were only occasional gusts of light wind. Although Maud had barely remembered the scenery until this point, she now recognized it in its entirety. All around her, she sensed the land, which rose in tiers—the fields, the farms, the villages, and the Dior—as if they were part of a permanent, harmonious order, guaranteed to outlast the humans, who only came and went in this small corner of the world. The incessant passing of creatures that inhabited the area made this eternity accessible to the soul. One felt it slowly, ardently, and sensitively unfolding, like a road forever warm with the steps of the last passersby and still with a silence forever hollowed out by the sound of steps to come and bodies on their way.

The road cut across the dark slope of the terrain. Immobile and milky white, it crossed the countryside, strangely absent, like a courier coming from afar who thinks only of his goal.

Although it was difficult to see anything, one could sense that many lives still carried on at night, now calmer and voiceless, yet existing more powerfully, perhaps, than during the day, which no longer dispersed them with its light. This was how Maud perceived The Pardal, perched on the summit of the incline, and below it the hamlet of Semoic, down by the Dior, which was murmuring with fresh and silky sounds.

Cries, distant noises, barking dogs, and the voices of young people calling to one another arrived isolated from their source and in a familiar way, as gentle to the ear as the sound of the sea.

Farmers had their supper early. They ate, no doubt, in a silence composed of tiredness and peace. They would soon go to bed, worn out by the fatigue of the day that had just gone by, and by the denser and heavier fatigue that imperceptibly swallowed up each day of their lives a bit more. And all the forms of tiredness that came together at the end of the day left certain fragrances in the air, those of the earth and of stone, which does not die, those of herds, and those of man, gentle and touching.

John Pecresse thought he would find Maud on the porch of the dining room. He came to join her there and, without saying a word, leaned up against the other side of the door. Maud was barely able to make him out now, done up in his hunting outfit, tall and a little thickset, like a man who is getting older, and not like the youngster she had known in the past. She thought about his life in this house, in the middle of this farmland that belonged to him and on which he lived with ease, without having to count the cost. He irritated her, because she felt he was always keyed up, concerned about the effect he was making, painfully forcing himself to appear something other than what he was.

John felt worried. "What effect does it have on her to be here, at my place, on the porch of the house from which one can see, far off, at least half of my lands bordering on Uderan and the Dior?" He blamed himself for the girl's silence; the feeling of a huge emptiness already overwhelmed him when he was near her. The mistresses that he had had by chance had always found him full of a trying sentimentality, but they attached very little importance to it because they were from the country and full of common sense; they let him both speak and write to them to his heart's content.

The Pecresse father left the stable and released his griffons, who took off like arrows in the black night. The dogs barked for quite a while, exasperated with joy and showing a child-like impatience. Even without seeing them, one could follow their pointless and disorganized comings and goings. Mrs. Taneran, Jacques, Henry, and Mrs. Pecresse also came out on the porch before dinner. Mrs. Taneran wanted to say something to Mrs. Pecresse in order to be friendly. "It feels good here; it feels better than Paris. The air is so fresh!"

Very pleased, Mrs. Pecresse agreed, answering in the same vein. Then no one said another word. Mr. Pecresse spoke to his dogs to keep them close to the house.

Maud heard Jacques yawning nervously behind her. Jacques! She thought of him suddenly with as much detachment as if he had been dead or absent for many years. For the first time in a long time, he was not in the familiar setting of their apartment. It was as if he had stopped living for a few days. He lost all interest and looked like an actor who is lifeless and superficial soon after the show.

The perspective of holidays bored Jacques. After one has taken a boat from Uderan down to the water mill of Mirasmes, what else is there to do in an area where small game is as rare as the girls? For ten years, his illusory existence had opened up new avenues of pleasure for him every day. Here, everything slipped away. The silence terrified him. He knew his mother's plans for him, but despite the fact that he had let himself be forced into a decision he now regretted, he told himself that it did not bind him in the least.

Like fog, boredom covered Jacques's life, and in this haze, reality faded and became elusive. He was very intelligent without ever having known the pleasures of the mind. His thought life, lazy as it was, never rose above his everyday preoccupations. It led him to his pleasures and then abandoned him, like the matchmaker who has fulfilled her duty. For a year he had given himself one reason to live: to hide the truth from his wife concerning the use of the money she had entrusted to him. He had no doubt held it against her that she was the source of his problems, without knowing it, and that had contributed to hastening the end of his love. It now spoiled his memories.

These memories, in reality, continued on in the form of payment dates from the Tavares Bank, which had to be respected no matter what. No doubt he did not love the deceased enough to suffer for a long time. Her death let him down because it no longer allowed him to hope for anything. He felt abandoned. All that was left was his empty heart and the statements from the bank.

The Pecresse father whistled for his griffons, who came regretfully into the house. The Tanerans and their hosts sat down to dinner later than usual. But even if the atmosphere picked up on account of the good food, the Pecresses remained vaguely worried and disconcerted by the Tanerans.

CHAPTER 5

MRS. PECRESSE WAS A SINGULAR WOMAN. AT THE PARDAL, SHE was looked on as a woman with a good head on her shoulders, and she was respected. Having only a few friends, however, she was concerned about people's opinion. She knew people criticized her in relation to her son, and even though she realized that the slander being spread in The Pardal was inspired by jealousy, she let herself be tormented by the unspoken worries it caused.

As soon as the Tanerans arrived, her concern grew. Although the idea of marriage had germinated in her mind prematurely, the feelings of her son for Maud Grant only confirmed it. She had never thought that there would be a link between marriage and the final acquisition of Uderan. Now this possibility arose in her mind in such an obvious way that she thought she had always foreseen it.

Even if the Grant-Tanerans were only bourgeois folk without distinction, Uderan, their land, conferred on them a kind of nobility. And it was precisely because the property was in a state of disrepair that Mrs. Pecresse wanted it so strongly. The prospect of action intoxicated this woman. She wanted to act and to drag her son John into the adventure. What could be more exciting than to join in a common cause with the one who is dear to you? No one ever knew how far this hope led Mrs. Pecresse and in what delectations it caused her to bask in advance.

But she knew how to put the brakes on her imagination, which had never blinded her. Her passion took on an air of reflection naturally and expressed itself skillfully. The only error to which she fell prey was to attribute to Maud Grant the value and attraction of the land the young woman possessed. Without having done any calculations, from one day to the next, Maud appeared worthy of Mrs. Pecresse's covetous ambitions for her son.

Even if Maud was not all that beautiful in the opinion of the Pardalians, did she not possess, in fact, traces of a race that was different from her own? She walked down the fruit path slowly, with an erect posture, without rushing, as if no one or nothing were waiting for her; no obligation bowed her down, except that of living life as it came. And Mrs. Pecresse, who attended to so many tasks that she wouldn't have known what to do with a moment of leisure, found in *that* the true mark of an essential difference. The fact that she thought Maud was of a superior quality to her flattered her modesty and kindled even more her desire to see Maud marry her son.

Soon all of The Pardal had made the inevitable connection: the Grant daughter, with nothing to do from morning till night, was certainly looking for a husband. And after all, it was better that a good man from The Pardal get that unculti-vated land in shape, especially because, of the Grant-Tanerans' two sons, one was too young and the other incompetent . . .

Mrs. Taneran sensed these calculations, or rather these hopes. She didn't want to displease either Mrs. Pecresse or the local farmers. Whenever she happened to be alone with her daughter, she kept herself from saying anything. But she had spoken about it to Jacques, as she always did with things concerning the family.

"So, who will you marry her to?" he had replied. "I'd be generous. I'd go away; I'd take a pass on the question of the land, which doesn't bring in any profit and loses value every year; Pecresse would pay me something . . ."

Perhaps he thought that a solution of this kind would arrange his affairs. But his mother, usually so weak, so ame-nable, dug in her heels. She claimed she would prefer to see Maud become an old maid than marry her to a Pecresse. Since her arrival, moreover, his mother was easy to irritate. When obliged to defend her child, she was surprised that she cared so strongly about Maud, who didn't show her any tender-ness. In contrast to the spinelessness of her sons, this reticence comforted her, especially recently, since she had noticed that Henry, too, was getting worse. This was why, in the face of the danger Mrs. Taneran was discovering, Maud seemed to be so disarmed and so innocent that her mother felt all her energy was necessary to save her daughter.

Soon the rumors were flying. People became emboldened, for, either thoughtlessly or because they found it so comfort-able, the Tanerans did not leave the Pecresse house for their own. Was it to give credibility to the general opinion? Mrs.

Pecresse suggested to the Tanerans that they give a dinner at Uderan itself for all the Pardalians.

In reality, Mrs. Pecresse feared that her idea was crazy. "If it is," she told herself, "I'll see it clearly that night by the way they act . . ."

Although she lived apart from the Pardalians, whose daughters seemed too commonplace for her heir, she clung to them now, because she suspected that her idea was not just the fruit of the imagination of a disillusioned woman. Her dream frightened her, considering that it might happen, and considering that she might see John beside Maud, in the yard or at the table. She entertained this dream and marveled at it like a young girl who has not yet begun to live in reality. "Things don't happen by themselves," she repeated to herself. "You have to act on them."

But nothing seemed to happen that was decisive or even seemed like the beginning of a realization. Thus, she naïvely put hope in this dinner . . .

Though they were already into May, they lit the fireplaces in all the main-floor rooms at Uderan two days in advance. The house lost some of its sad, musty smell. There was still one room somewhat inhabitable, furnished with a canopy-covered bed, too bulky to have been moved. Beside the big bed was another, a child's bed, left because it was not usable. Maud, as a little girl, and then Henry had slept there. This room was at the extreme edge of the grounds, at the end of a pathway of linden trees. One of its walls overlooked an old greenhouse, which, for as long as anyone could recall, had been abandoned and left to hobos, who often spent the night there when passing through the region.

Maud decided to sleep at Uderan. Mrs. Dedde arranged the bedroom for her. Although Mrs. Taneran found Maud's idea a bit preposterous, she didn't remark on it. She let Maud do what she wanted, showing her incredible leniency . . .

It was decided that the Pecresses' son would accompany Maud to Uderan that same evening. Having become extremely considerate, John guided her along the narrow road with a hurricane lamp, and she preceded him in the stream of light cast by the lantern. She wanted to thank him but didn't find anything to say.

They had almost arrived when John Pecresse made the effort to ask her, "My mother hasn't said anything to you, Maud Grant?"

Maud was unaware of all the intrigue that swirled around her. When she turned around, she saw his worried eyes shining. "No, nothing! I don't know what she could have said to me. Good-bye. No need to go any farther. I know the road here, because from the hedge on we're at Uderan. When I was little, I never went any farther. Thank you anyway . . ."

She went on her way. He was stupefied for a moment, but then ran back. His mother, who must have been following the light of the lamp, closed the shutters of her bedroom with such force that the din went as far as Maud. Mrs. Pecresse had no doubt put a lot of hope in this walk. It was her first disappointment, and her nervousness kept her from sleeping for a long time . . .

Maud, for her part, felt reassured as soon as she reached the grounds. She walked briefly down the pathways that crossed the premises and came back gently. The silence, which would have made anyone else flee, dense and mysterious as it was, enchanted her instead. Around her, the huge box hedges bristled, the pine trees took on gigantic proportions, and their summits wept gently, even though their moaning spread no sadness.

Maud heard her heart beating curiously at a certain point, as if it had been outside her chest. She heard it and made out another sound farther away that mixed with her heartbeat, sometimes becoming very perceptible and sometimes getting lost in the night, depending on the whims of the wind. With her hand on her chest, she held her breath. The noise soon plunged into the sunken road and circumvented the high, dark cliff formed by the grounds on that side.

"It's a horse . . . ," she said to herself. "I don't know anyone around here who has one. The farmers at Uderan don't know how to ride a horse . . ."

When the horse and rider drew near, she remained motionless, as if the stranger, in merely sensing her presence, might have felt wary. She knew nothing of him but decided he was courageous because he wasn't moving any more quickly than he had been before arriving at this road, which was black like an oven and overhung with tightly knit hedgerows. For an instant, Maud seemed to be attached to the hoofbeats, which descended toward the village. Once they reached the main road, they became clearer. Then no other noise troubled the silence, in which they left a kind of sound trail that seemed to fade with difficulty.

Maud went back into the house, leaving the large front door open to the grounds, which the light of the moon was probing. But the breeze that had earlier revealed the passing of the stranger kept her from sleeping for a long time. Maud fell asleep as soon as the breeze died down of itself in the forest, as if it had lost its strength, but she woke up abruptly as soon as a fresh breath of wind carrying all the surrounding fragrances returned and made the curtains shudder. It had swept the great depths of the valley, carrying with it, as a result, the scent of bitter algae and decayed leaves.

CHAPTER 6

THE DOOR OF THE LARGE DINING ROOM AT UDERAN HAD been left open. The day workers and tenant farmers were eating in the kitchen. Their wives and daughters served the meal, barely finding a minute, here and there, to eat themselves. They brought out the dishes, their mouths full, their foreheads damp with perspiration, flushed and happy with their exhaustion, which wasn't the same as their everyday fatigue.

In the dining room, the notables and farmers lined each side of the long table in a dignified fashion. The latter, being landowners of The Pardal, were born there and would probably die there; in their view, the tenant farmers were of an inferior status, similar to that of mercenaries who worked the land. Thus, being conscious of the respect being paid to the permanence and stability of their own condition, the farmers sat there proudly, although a little awkwardly, in their best clothes. In total, there were at least thirty who had come as a group. Under their eyelids, creased by the sun, they wore a mocking look, showing that they mainly regarded this invitation as the windfall of a good meal. Certainly, they would never have thought of doing this themselves. At the time of the grape harvests, when the people of The Pardal went to one another's places to eat, it was always with the expectation of something to be done in return, usually the exchange of a few days of work; but of course, you didn't just invite people over for nothing, for the pleasure of it . . .

At the beginning of the meal, they felt ill at ease, and even if some of the bolder ones tried to make a few jokes, they got little back for their efforts. The noise they made in loudly slurping their soup barely made up for the seemingly endless silence.

Caught up with the scene, Maud clearly recalled a past as lasting and inalterable as the features of their faces, which for the most part had not changed. Despite the efforts made to gain her attention by the young Pecresse, seated near her, she remained distracted.

At each end of the table, two big oil lamps lit up the guests who presided over the dinner. Mrs. Taneran chatted with the pharmacist of The Pardal, a big man whose hands appeared pale in comparison with the sun-scorched hands of the farmers. On the other side, in the middle, in consideration of his status, was the schoolteacher of The Pardal. His former pupil Henry Taneran, placed at his left, interacted with him with as much feigned or naïve sweetness as before, when he was a child.

It wasn't long before everyone started talking with his neighbor, although no one dared speak to the whole group yet. In the growing buzz of the conversation, one could pick out a few asides muttered in the thick dialect of the Dordogne area.

The Pecresse mother, sitting at Maud's right, was twisting and turning with nervousness. From time to time, she murmured a few words to her son, who immediately started in on Maud with his stuffy politeness. But his nasal voice, covered up by the other voices, failed to hold Maud's attention.

The rowdiness grew. When it got to be a terrible racket, with people raising their voices as loudly as they could, the din became deafening and monotonous, and yet Maud was no more overwhelmed than the night before, in the tremendous quiet of the grounds.

They were all there around the table, stingy, lumbering, unsociable workers, from the tall, good-natured Pellegrain, whose colossal stature dominated the crowd, right down to Dedde, the short tenant farmer. But they knew how to have fun by alluding to something or telling a story. To loosen up their tongues, which were usually tied (as if speaking during the week were a sin), the wine of Uderan worked wonders—a white wine, a bit dry, that had taken on the mineral taste of the plateau. Mr. Dedde had kept it for ten years, it seemed, in readiness for the return of the Tanerans; with time it had acquired a deep and treacherous sweetness. As rough as they were, the farmers tasted the wine with finesse; after each swig, they sniffed it and claimed they would have recognized it anywhere; they compared it to this or that other wine and gave advice to Dedde: "Be careful. You shouldn't let it age for more than five years. It's delicate—you may lose it."

After they had begun, it became a sparring match in which each one claimed some authority the others didn't have, launching into nuances that would have seemed insignificant to the uninitiated. At the end of an hour, however, there was a bit of a lull in the conversation, as they began to lack for topics.

"Now they're going to start talking about Uderan," thought Maud. They were going to repeat stories she knew word for word, which would serve to tie together scenes that the customary progress of their jubilation or state of well-being called to mind, one by one.

"Do you remember, Maud?" one of the men began . . . "Maud, someone's speaking to you! Do you remember the terrible fear you had, ten years ago . . . ?"

She gave a start. What was happening? Everyone was looking at her. Mrs. Pecresse, at her right, and John Pecresse were overjoyed to have drawn all the guests' attention toward her. Everyone was quiet, suddenly ashamed that they had shown a lack of propriety by forgetting to turn the conversation toward Miss Grant that night. Mrs. Taneran, for her part, was annoyed at the stupefaction one could read in her daughter's eyes. As for her brothers, they shrugged their shoulders in a barely noticeable way, whose meaning only she could guess. "What an idiot!" was what it meant. "What I think about it is just for the family!"

When Maud answered at last, a bit of defiance punctuated each of her words. "Oh, I remember! But there's a lot you don't know. Picture this! It happened one day when I was bringing back the cows from the field by the Dior and the train went by in the middle of the herd. Brownie was left with a huge red hole in place of one of her horns, and she pooped and bellowed. My teeth were chattering with fear. You thought I was very courageous. But after the accident,

I spent the night crying, because they were going to put the animal down. You're the one that told me, Alexis, that evening. You were drunk, but I believed you anyway."

Alexis, who had the head of a Gascon, with a narrow mustache, blushed with delight at hearing his name mentioned, but, recalling his drinking binges, everyone made fun of him. Mercilessly, Maud continued, finding a cruel pleasure in her words. Why did she persist this way?

"Christmas night, do you remember, Alexis? It was in the woods at the Paulins'. You were lying in the mud, hanging on to your shotgun as if it would actually keep you from falling into an abyss. We bumped into you with our feet and you hollered like a crazy man. Was it the cold that got you fired up like that, eh, Alexis?"

"Yes, Miss Grant," he answered, his eyes pleading with her.

But the others now sided instinctively with Alexis. They all felt exposed by the subtle irony of this girl who until now had remained silent and all at once showed herself to be so aggressive. What she said baffled and embarrassed them at the same time. So Maud gave up that approach from that point on, and only joined in the conversation to liven it up, giving a word of praise or approval here or there that would cause people to listen to the person with whom she was talking. She already knew the weight of her smile, of her attentive look, and immediately they were grateful for the goodwill that she showed.

Little by little, the gaiety died down, as it had come. Everyone pushed his or her chair out from the table. The fires that had half died down were crackling, and, to ward off any omens, the Deddes' daughter extinguished them completely with the poker . . .

The dress of flowered cotton that Maud was wearing, which appeared a little faded in the glimmer of the lamps, distinguished her from the farm women, who were still wrapped up in their woolen garb. It occurred to the young woman that once the hearths had been extinguished, the cold coming from the other rooms would slowly invade the big dining room. Gradually, even though they had had a lot to drink, the guests would soon be on their way. Thus, she threw another armful of vine shoots into the fireplace, and the fire, in a sudden burst, began purring again, devouring the dry twigs.

All of a sudden, she pricked up her ears. Although silence seemed to reign over the grounds and the whole Uderan domain, she knew before anyone else that it had just been broken. The same gallop she had perceived the night before came to her distinctly, and from the same direction. Soon the noise was so obvious that everyone stopped talking to listen to it.

"It's George Durieux," declared the young Pecresse. "I can imagine the look he'll have on his face when he sees the windows lit up. It's certainly the first time in years."

"Where's he going like that?" asked Maud.

"Who knows? It depends on the one he's with at the moment. For now, it's Semoic."

"Oh, that's it," said Mrs. Pecresse, shaking her head back and forth. And right away her son imitated her gesture, which said everything.

Mrs. Taneran was anxious to have some details on George Durieux.

"A fellow from Bordeaux. He bought back a piece of property near Semoic and comes here on holidays. You know, the one you can't see from the road. There's a long pathway of cypress trees that leads to it. He wanted something in the region because his father had lived here for a long time; he even thought of buying Uderan."

"Hallo, Mr. Durieux!" The parish priest had opened the window, and everyone was astonished to see that the rider was already in the yard, holding his horse by its bridle.

"I thought I was dreaming," the rider shouted. "From the top of the road I could see the lights of Uderan."

He finished tying up his animal and came into the room. He was a tall, dark-haired man who didn't appear to Maud to be particularly good-looking. His careless dress highlighted instead a native elegance that struck one immediately because of the ease of his movements, which showed off a dexterity like that of an animal. He seemed a bit dazzled, with the expression on his face passing from indifference to a childlike curiosity. He looked at everyone attentively, spoke to them in a friendly way, but didn't listen to them very long and seemed after a moment or so not to notice them anymore. From his first glance, he had fixed all the attendees in his mind and could easily pick out the landowners, even though he was far from knowing everyone in The Pardal. His politeness tinged with disdain once again gave people a sense of their social standing; sensitive to his charm, Mrs. Taneran gave such a feminine smile as soon as he entered that she appeared younger. With the arrival of George Durieux, moreover, the real meaning of the gathering appeared to Maud as an unbearable, self-evident fact.

"She's the one people in the area are talking about and who may end up staying at Uderan," the stranger must have thought. "One of these nights this lout will take her to his place, with her mother wishing they had gotten away. They must be seriously short of money . . ."

Maud lifted her eyes. They were a very light gray. Her look quickly met that of the young man, a look as clear as hers and hardened by the same will, but more practiced. In speaking, he didn't stop staring at her. When he realized that people noticed, he turned away for a few minutes, but almost immediately began again. However, he didn't stop talking.

"Every day," he said to Mrs. Taneran, "I ride along the side of your property, madame"—he stressed these words as if he were mocking her—"and I know it very well. Your vines, on the side of the Pellegrains', especially the big one that spreads out over the two slopes of the plateau, are not worth much anymore, unfortunately. It's useless to fertilize them. All that's left is to tear them out!"

"I thought," argued the tall Pellegrain, "that by grafting them . . . " Soon everyone came to the rescue, that is, those of The Pardal. The Pecresses murmured something in their corner, wanting to play their part as well. What George Durieux was saying did not disadvantage people's interests directly, but they felt nevertheless that their collective faith in the value of Uderan was shaken.

"No, believe me," the young man continued, "except for burning the whole plateau and then replanting . . . But what good would that do—isn't that true, madame? You never come here. When you bought it, it was already depleted to the maximum. It's been like that for decades. You can't do anything but leave Uderan as it is. Woe to the person who tries to change something. The region is infested with ruined landowners who used to own your domain. There's no one but you, farmers of The Pardal, who hold on to hope for this desolate land . . ."

Mrs. Taneran continued smiling blissfully for no obvious reason . . .

"You see," he continued, "this soil is so impoverished that you would have to invest a fortune in it to make up for lost time. Furthermore, one can live very well at Uderan, in a sense, provided that one asks of it only what it can give: a few cuttings of wood, some fruit, some fodder."

Apparently he wanted to discourage the desire of the people of The Pardal to acquire the land. Was he lying? He expressed himself with a gentle indifference that would have fooled the most discerning, but that contrasted with the intensity of his look. When he felt that the disillusionment had begun to undermine their point of view, he spoke to them about other things. Today, moreover, he had almost won the match. Tomorrow, certainly, with the day's dawning, when they would once more cross Uderan bathed in mists, the desire to possess it would seize them again. George knew that, but for tonight, it was enough to have put a dent in their covetousness.

John Pecresse, on the other hand, didn't really care what George Durieux had to say. He believed that he loved Maud, but in reality found himself as much a stranger to her as George Durieux, for his part, appeared already to be part of her private life. Effectively, Maud listened to the words of the latter with passionate interest. The dancing light of the fire dug shadows under her slight shoulders, and her face possessed a beauty that Pecresse felt confusedly escaped him. Besides killing his desire, this revelation drove him to despair. Unconsciously, he held it against his mother for defending what she called her interests with such vulgarity. From that evening on, he knew he was defeated in advance, but he understood how dangerous it would have been to let Maud see it, for although she wasn't cruel, she looked at him with empty eyes as soon as he tried to speak of himself, as if she had been struck with an insurmountable stupidity. He felt he could no longer stand the presence of Durieux and stood up.

He left. His mother followed him automatically, while her heart, like his, was overcome with anguish and vague worry. Everyone from The Pardal left behind them, as an apparent protest. But basically, people just felt tired, as happens naturally after a late evening out.

CHAPTER 7

DURING THE TWO WEEKS THAT FOLLOWED THE DINNER, George Durieux dropped in to Uderan almost every day. These days, which appeared to be so similar, were marked by unpleasant periods of waiting for Maud. In the afternoon, Mrs. Taneran went to Uderan in order to organize things she had left behind the last time and wanted to take back to Paris. Although she was always up and about in the city, she claimed that her nerves had collapsed, and most of the time, worn out in advance at the idea of furnishing the least bit of effort, she would stretch out in the easy chair on the lawn that separated the yard from the vegetable garden. There, in the warm, checkered shade of an arbor, she would sometimes sleep.

Maud, during the afternoon, would be on the lookout for George Durieux. After a few days she realized something that didn't surprise her at all: Jacques, who was bored, was also waiting for the young man.

As different as the Grants and Tanerans were from each other, and as different as their passions were, an identical tendency in each of their natures caused them to resemble each other: the friend of one, unless he was repelled by the role (and in that case they quickly lost interest in listening or speaking to him), became, shortly after his entrance into the clan, the confidant of the whole family. Each time a new person appeared, having been brought in by one or the other, a kind of communicative passion caused each of them to warm up to him in their own way and to try to monopolize him. But soon the newcomer, perceiving that in reality an irresolvable conflict reigned among the family members, was obliged to choose. If he took one side or the other, he would experience singular moments and the illusion of arbitrating in an exceptionally unjust and fascinating situation, filling him with enthusiasm and causing him to experience, for a time, heroic ecstasy. Then, very rapidly, he realized that nobody put forth any goodwill toward reconciliation. So while he thought he had arranged everything, those involved escaped him, and for reasons he was unable to grasp. It was then up to him to make the effort to adjust once again to the rhythm, ultimately monotonous, of this kind of perpetual movement of discord and heartrending emotion. Most of the time, he got tired of it. Thus, the Grant-Tanerans didn't have any real friends and found themselves, at the end of the day, still alone.

Durieux ignored the fact that it was in this context that they were waiting for him at Uderan. Though he seemed to be losing interest in Maud, he quite often stopped at the domain anyway.

Sitting on a pine-tree branch that was hewn in the shape of a bench and easy to reach, Maud read absentmindedly. At the end of the yard, Jacques, in shirtsleeves, was working on a flower bed that overlooked the road. (He had decided to stay at Uderan. His friendship with Durieux no doubt counted for a lot in this unexpected decision.) Mrs. Taneran, happy to see her son working at something, if only a child's task, concluded magnanimously that "basically, he had always had a love for the earth."

Except for a few little clashes with Mrs. Pecresse since their arrival at Uderan, Maud noticed that things were turning out better for her family than she had expected.

Jacques didn't seem worried, except during breakfast at the Pecresse home, when the mailman came. On leaving Paris, he had asked the concierge to send back the letters from the Tavares Bank, for fear that the family be discovered and that he be harassed once again. But after a couple of weeks, of course, the letters arrived in a pile—warning letters with bailiff fees. Mrs. Taneran lent her son a considerable sum. After that there was silence, which should have worried Jacques, but he thought he had been forgotten. Pleased with this lull and doing better, he showed a politeness toward everyone that he rarely used in Paris.

He would dig without lifting his head, while Henry was fishing with his chums on the banks of the Dior. From time to time, they would joyfully announce what they had caught. Jacques didn't stop digging except to reply. And Mrs. Taneran, who was afraid that it looked as if she were dozing off, would call out in a voice laden with sleep, "Don't stay in the shade! It's chilly and unhealthy. Do you hear, Maud?"

The passing of the two trains from Bordeaux was the big event of the day. George came by after the first and, in the space of two weeks, had never come by after the second.

Between the two, the time that passed was inestimable. They waited for George. In the dry air, the sounds came as far as the grounds, taking on the aura of their successive echoes in the woods and valleys, and in the humid shadow of the pine woods, it felt as if they were witnessing the magic of summer.

Sometimes the local train cruelly thwarted Maud's expectations and reminded her of the possibility that George might not come. Before the second train passed, John Pecresse would arrive, all out of breath, coming from the Dior right up to the pine tree where Maud was sitting.

Like a good farmer, he judged the Grant-Tanerans to be weak and frivolous, but he did his best to live as they did in order to gain Maud's confidence. Since the arrival of his neighbors, he didn't work as hard in the fields and lamentably hung around with Henry and his bunch of friends, who were much younger than John. "Come on," he said to Maud, "we're all going to the mill, and then we'll take a ride in Terry's car—hurry up!"

"Is it Henry who sent you?" asked Maud distrustfully.

"No," he replied, "but he won't mind. If I'm speaking softly, it's because of Jacques . . . If he comes, it's all over. Come on, hurry up, I'm pleading with you . . ."

Sometimes, in his impatience, John pulled on her ankles, while in the valley Henry rallied his buddies and called the young man with a worried voice.

"I'm not interested! Let go of me or you'll be sorry," she warned, sending him away brutally.

Once, she had broken into an irritated laugh, so unexpected that Jacques threatened to come and get involved. John had known Maud since her childhood and still acted with her in childish ways that allowed him to approach her more easily than he otherwise should have. She jostled him in such a rough yet familiar way that he couldn't get angry, becoming, with each passing day, more eager and more forceful toward her.

George arrived on foot or on horseback, according to his mood. As soon as he turned onto the road, Jacques would call to him, "Could you come here a moment? I'm almost done. Could we go down together?"

Before going down to Semoic with his friend, George climbed the stairs, pushed open the small gate, and walked under the pine tree. There he lifted his head, his hands in his pockets, but without ever stopping. Then he walked back up the grounds, toward the esplanade, whistling or coughing discreetly before reaching Mrs. Taneran, so that she would wake up without being embarrassed that he had found her napping.

Maud, who had been waiting for hours, forced herself to remain calm with such an effort of the will that it destroyed the pleasure she should have felt. She jumped from her bench and walked slowly toward the esplanade. A sort of inner obligation pushed her every day to make this useless move toward George.

"Can you imagine that, Mr. Durieux? My daughter always stays there under the pine tree, in the shade. As if there weren't a thousand things to do in the country!"

Jacques shrugged his shoulders and, without meaning to, diverted the suspicions that could have been directed toward George in regard to Maud. "It's a style she wants to give herself. She's sentimental; she wants to be noticed."

Maud's eyelids fluttered very slightly, changing the immobility of her face. She sat down on the bench that ran along the kitchen wall, somewhat away from the group. George Durieux, held back by Mrs. Taneran, took a seat on the chair she now had the habit of bringing him.

He intentionally avoided addressing the young woman, and she understood that he would have liked to do so. He hesitated to look at her, as if prevented by an actual impediment, and each time his eyes met Maud's, he turned away, disturbed. To give himself some composure, he played with the first cherries that had fallen from the tree, still green. He grouped them in twos, then threes, examining them attentively without appearing to see them, then, with his fingernails, carving them up one by one. His black, shiny hair was parted in big tufts, like heavy grass that the wind blows flat and gathers up into bunches that show, long afterward, traces of the storm. Despite the short-sleeved shirt he wore, his long body could be made out in its entirety by the color of his arms, by their lean, oblong form, and by that of his nervous ankles, where the tendons moved visibly under the skin.

One could sense that he was young and agile in his movements, but always ready to indulge in laziness or pleasure. His relaxed attitude and limber body captivated people, drawing them to him. In his face, which reflected a childlike gentleness, his eyes remained alert, curious about everything Mrs. Taneran was telling him. Though intelligent, he had to take the trouble to speak in order for people to judge for themselves; he never forced himself to please others, which is why he managed to do it naturally, and why people around him made an effort to seek out his friendship. He liked to swim in the Dior, to hunt, and to have a roaring good time all night long at Semoic.

"I wounded a rabbit just above your woods this morning," he said. "It's the Deddes' dog that probably got it. In fact, I saw their daughter, who told me something I didn't know." He had turned toward Jacques, who, impatient to leave with him, kept getting up from his bench. "You're planning to move in to Uderan."

"One of my mother's ideas, my friend. I just go along with it." He laughed, but deep down, he was bothered by the way people were astonished when it came to him. His biting tone of voice made it clear that if people were expecting him to settle down, they would be more than disappointed. But George's tone, simple and natural, calmed his suspicions. Jacques began again, with studied politeness. "The tenant farmhouse is charming, with its steps between every room. It's more cheerful than here, so that's where I'll stay. We'll be closer to each other."

"Yes, it's much nicer," agreed Mrs. Taneran, "especially because the Deddes will take care of him when we're away. Have you heard anything about the tenant house, Mr. Durieux?"

"People say it's very old and has lasted more years than all the homes of The Pardal put together. It was joined to Uderan a long time after its construction. My father could give you all the information you need on it. In fact . . ."

Jacques got up. "Are you going down to Semoic, Durieux?" Not as tall as George, Jacques was good-looking in a more harmonious way, thanks to his well-proportioned body, even though he was still lacking his beautiful brown sheen of summers gone by.

At Semoic, thought Maud, a following was probably building up around them, fatally. Now, every evening they went down there together, and even though Jacques had proposed this outing to George in an indifferent tone, one felt that nothing would have kept him from it . . .

A similarity existed between George and her brother, and Maud discerned it from the nuances, the unspoken complicity between them. "You're going to Semoic?"

George got up from his chair, all the while continuing to talk to Jacques. "I hope that if you make up your mind to spend some money and fix up your tenant farm, it won't be because of the superstitions flying around. As far as I'm concerned, I'm delighted. I'm here until October every year, and sometimes at Christmas I come back to hunt."

At last Mrs. Taneran got up and smoothed out her dress with the back of her hand. Maud felt no joy in seeing George, because he remained so indifferent. In her silent confrontation, she employed all the willpower of a woman who has decided to triumph at all costs over a refusal for which she has no explanation. She applied herself to the task without pride. Keeping George from leaving for a few moments, prolonging her torture, attached him to her even more, without his knowing it.

Thus, she made a last attempt to keep the conversation going. "You don't believe the superstitions spread around by the farmers?" Everyone turned around. Mrs. Taneran smiled.

George took on a mocking tone in addressing her. "Of course not. Why? Do you believe them? People around here claim, anyway, that you have no fear."

Jacques grabbed George by the arm. "It's because she always sleeps here alone, so she'll get noticed. She gets even more credit because these frightening tales are flying around. Do you understand?"

George looked at the ground like someone who is remembering something, and broke into laughter. "That reminds me of a ridiculous story I'll tell you someday."

Maud tried one last time to grab the interest of the young men. "But who says, *who* says that I'm not afraid?"

"Don't mind her, Mr. Durieux. She's both nervous and shy . . ." The two women accompanied the visitor down to the gate.

The second train whistled. A car flew by the property on the way to Semoic. While they were expressing their astonishment and wondering who the crazy driver was, Maud identified him as Henry's friend Terry. Jacques, who refrained from uttering an insult out of respect for George, whom he didn't know well enough yet, pointed out that the car could have stopped to pick them up, knowing they were going down to Semoic.

They left. While Mrs. Taneran closed up the house, Maud stretched out on the grass surrounding a bush of wild roses, suddenly worn out by such a long wait.

The afternoon was coming to an end. No more sounds came from the valley except, occasionally, the loud calls of the Deddes' daughter, who took the cows down to drink in the ponds of the Dior meadow when those on the plateau were dried up.

The birds were putting down for the night; they filled the grounds with their cries, mellow with tiredness. Mrs. Taneran reappeared. "Did you say, Maud, that your brother Henry left with Terry? I'm afraid of an accident. Do you know why they all go to Semoic?"

Maud didn't know. Mrs. Taneran once again slowed down the moment of departure, walking along the short, broad paths that wound around the grounds. In the evening at Uderan, the slightest sound impressed her, whether a footstep on the road or the echo of an oar on the Dior. "What's that? Listen, Maud . . ." As they listened, everything seemed inhabited with strange sounds, especially the empty house.

Soon the roses became purple, and a color like that of blood began to rise around the clumps of trees. "It's strange, as soon as evening comes, I wouldn't stay here for anything in the world," said the mother. "It's true you have courage, Maud!"

Oh, what did these words matter, because George was no longer there . . . ? Maud felt that if George got along so well with her brother, it was because they resembled each other in a certain aspect of their nature. The same fundamental laziness and their penchant for pleasure drew them together.

Finally Mrs. Taneran joined up with Maud on the side of the hill, near the flowers. "What's the matter? Are you sick? Let's get going. I'm not saying that I enjoy going back to the Pecresses'; we should never have moved in there. But now it's too late to leave there and too soon to come back. Your brothers are making the most of being in the countryside."

She wanted to share her sacrifice with her daughter, in order to show her affection. Since the life of the family no longer weighed her down as much, she suffered from being neglected by her children . . .

One evening when they were together, loud knocks at the entrance gate on the side of the vegetable garden startled them. Soon the knocking was so forceful they felt afraid. Without answering, they descended the side of the hill toward the metal gate. But when they opened it, the voice of Mrs. Pecresse, sugary and familiar, calmed them down. "I thought you were at the tenant farm. I came looking for you to talk a bit on the way home." In a few seconds Mrs. Taneran got over her fear, and turning toward her daughter with her usual authority, she ordered, "Go home by the main road, and above all don't worry."

Boredom reigned at Uderan—dense and oppressive. In order not to slow down their arrival at the Barque Inn in Semoic, Jacques Grant preferred to meet George Durieux midway between the village and the property. For this reason the latter came to Uderan less and less frequently. The last time had been two weeks earlier, and it was on this occasion that he seemed to be interested in Maud.

"Every summer I organize a fishing party for crayfish. I'd like to have the three of you with me. I'll let you know when," he had said. His cordial tone indicated that he owed a certain politeness to the Tanerans and that he was simply fulfilling his duty. Since that time, he had not come back to the estate; he took the loop of The Pardal to connect with the road to Semoic and also avoided taking the shortcut across the property. Clearly, he was withdrawing from their company, and it seemed unimaginable they would see him again someday.

Mrs. Taneran, who greatly missed him, was worried. "How is it that we don't see Durieux anymore? Is he still going to Barque's?" Then, noticing that Jacques now left for Semoic without waiting for his friend, she vehemently reproached him. "Your sister and I are dying of boredom here. You've taken away the least bit of company from us, as usual. If I see Durieux I'll tell him what I think."

Mrs. Taneran did nothing at Uderan. Her lack of activity had become all the more unsupportable because not only Mrs. Pecresse, but all the Pardalians, kept her at a disdainful distance, as much because of her own attitude toward her neighbors as because of that of her son. But Jacques had laughed at his mother's reproaches. "You think he enjoyed coming here! He just came to be polite, poor Durieux. You're wrong about people; you don't know what kind of man he is, that Durieux . . ."

At the end of her patience, Maud finally stopped spending her afternoons in the yard, and, to give herself some purpose, she went looking for the Deddes' daughter, who kept the cows near the Riotor. But the tenant farmer's daughter, whom she questioned somewhat obliquely, revealed very little about George. The Deddes' daughter also frequented Barque's. "You should come, Miss Grant. What's nice there is that nobody pays any attention to you. I'm taking advantage of it before winter." But Maud was no more inclined to go there than she was to come out of her habitual solitude.

They began to rearrange the three rooms of the tenant farmer's home where Jacques was going to live, and Maud helped a little, although she didn't like finding herself with her mother, whose recent, inexplicable tenderness embarrassed her (she didn't know what Mrs. Pecresse could have told her, the evening she knocked at the gate, but Maud had avoided coming back to their neighbor's until later that evening, at mealtime, in order not to be alone with her mother).

And soon, judging that it was even more worthless to take care of her brother's affairs than to wander around, she did nothing.

Toward the middle of June it rained for a week. The Deddes' daughter no longer took the cows out. Jacques's furniture arrived from Bordeaux, but it was impossible to go and get it at the Semoic train station because the weather was so bad. The persistent rain clogged up the roads and fell listlessly in sudden bursts. On the hillside streaming with water, the grass was crushed, beaten down and licked by numerous rivulets. Maud gave up walking in that area.

They didn't know where Henry was, whereas Jacques, finding it more convenient to live in his new quarters, slept there until it was time to leave for Semoic.

The farmers were upset with the rain. "It's bad for the plums," they moaned. "It takes away their taste . . ."

At Barque's, however, everything continued at a lively pace, according to the Deddes' daughter. The bad weather benefited the owner and attracted more and more people to his place. Maud, wearing a cape borrowed from the tenant farmer's daughter, roamed the roads and lanes, trying to meet up with George. This incessant searching took up entire days, right up until evening, and soon became a personal obligation, although she never fully understood that she was no longer expecting much from her search.

She didn't hold it against her brother in the least for monopolizing the man she loved. Fate had decided it. What could she do, in fact, against a form of seduction that always astonished her? In her brother's circles, passions were always being ignited and then quenched, and someone was always absorbed by them. She could guess the reasons why her brother monopolized George, because they were the same ones that drew her to him: first of all, his shameless desire, like Jacques, to live the way he wanted to, half farmer, half delinquent. He gave you the feeling of scoring a victory if you succeeded in pleasing him. Neither Jacques nor George had an occupation, but Maud thought it would have been deplorable to see George tied up by some kind of job. If he loved her, one day he would devote all his moments, all his leisure time, to her . . .

One afternoon, she got a glimpse of him. He passed by next to her, dressed like a farmer, in a velvet vest, looking down, with his hands in his pockets and his features drawn and weary, unaware of the fact that Maud was observing him from behind the hawthorn bushes. Wasn't he as far removed from thinking about her as she imagined him to be concerned with her? Under the endless rain, it must have been his own life, rather, that filled him with anxiety, and, as different as he was from Jacques, he resembled him, by virtue of the same battered look on his face brought on by the same kind of disgust.

Instead of bringing her joy, this apparition filled Maud with concern, and she didn't take a single step to meet him. But as soon as he disappeared down the road, she regretted her cowardice. She ran as fast as she could across the fields, where her shoes got bogged down like noisy suction cups, and along the Riotor, which swept muddy water along, right up to the edge of its banks. The pressing desire to end the sinister drama of her love kept her on tenterhooks.

At the tenant farmer's home, she found her mother sitting alone in an empty room, moaning. "I'm losing my mind, Maud. Can you believe that the furniture hasn't arrived and Jacques isn't looking after it any more than we are?" She noticed the expression on the face of her daughter, who was weeping nervously, like someone who is trying to keep from sobbing. Mrs. Taneran wasn't overly surprised.

"It's this weather, and I don't know what it is we feel here; I'm worried, too, as if something were about to happen . . ." And then, reflecting a bit, she commented, "If you're too bored, I can tell Henry to take you along with him . . ."

Around the tenant farm, the rain was falling straight down like hail. On the dark green pond, whose surface was riddled with raindrops, the two grindstones, already on their last legs, projected their shadows. The rain still pointed to summer's nonchalance, expressing its opulence in the swollen foliage, the intense, impenetrable heat, and the fallen fruit that covered the paths with its freshly rotting flesh. Under the porch awning, the light perfume of honeysuckle filled the air with its fragrance, mixed with the odor of the wet sandstone and the subtle, slightly salted savor of the shower. In the distance, the roof of Uderan displayed its numerous chimneys, majestically framed by the tops of the pinewood.

But little by little the storm lost its strength. Soon the rain fell only in light bursts. The sky cleared; the exertion of the clouds in the sky took on a calmer appearance. Here and there, in the middle, the sky opened up to an intense and brilliant blue that one might have called wet.

At the end of the afternoon, a white vapor coming from the oak woods and the Pellegrain plateau descended gently along the Riotor. It raced toward the Dior valley, where it would soon blend with a thick fog. The Dedde girl exited the barn with a basket on her arm and headed to the west field, toward The Pardal, to pick some vegetables. "When the mist descends like that, it's because the bad weather is over. Look how beautiful it is. On the other side you can hardly see," she said to Maud.

The tall poplars of the Riotor, frosted by the mist, stood still as she passed by. The estate found itself isolated from the surrounding region, which seemed to melt into the fog.

Mrs. Taneran came out of the house, headed toward the pond, and stood in front of the hollow road that remained the only way out toward the main route. She was nervous and murmured with a sigh, "Who knows where your brothers are? In an hour we won't be able to see anything with this fog, and Henry's out roaming the roads in Terry's car. I prefer not to know."

Maud had the desire, after this break, to stretch her legs. "I'm going to the main road to see if he's fishing on the banks of the Dior."

She put her hooded cape back on and took to the road with a quick step. It was true, she had forgotten the cause of her apprehension a bit earlier. In the weather's emerging calm, the memory of George softened and lost some of its importance.

Perhaps the man's indifference had seemed so insurmountable that she had given up hope. Why, following the dinner at Uderan, had she persuaded herself so easily that he would seek her out? Even if, for a few moments, he had looked at her, she had to be crazy to jump to the conclusion that he loved her. And then, perhaps she had also behaved awkwardly during his visits . . .

When she got to the road, she was surprised by the silence that had followed the outburst of the storm in the Dior valley. One would think oneself to be in the bottom of a damp well. "Henry!" Her voice reverberated in a brief echo that was unrecognizable. With no desire to return to the tenant farm, she sat down on a border stone at the corner of the property. "He's at Barque's, too," she thought.

Beside her, with enormous jolts, the trees shed the water weighing down their branches, though Maud could perceive no particular cause for their sudden upheavals. Soon a kind of gentle babbling emerged from the silence. Rivulets slid down the hill to the road, crossing at Maud's feet with twists and turns.

Maud realized that she was no longer thinking about George. Frightened by what she thought to be her fickleness, she determined to go to Barque's that very evening and was comforted by her decision.

After a moment, she called out for her brother again. A silence, as hard to break through as a wall would have been, responded to her call, while on the grounds the same fairylike sounds of water continued to play. Listening to them, Maud thought she heard sweet, melodious voices. "I'll go all the way to the Dior," she told herself, "but it will soon be night." She firmly resisted fear.

In the elm enclosure, at the corner of the field along the border of their property, Maud had once played. The memory suddenly came back to her: at ten years old she had played with Henry and Louise Rivière every Thursday. Taneran would come to lovingly watch his little boy. He wore an old khaki jacket and his hunting gaiters and already looked old, even then. When Jacques arrived, he would chase away his stepfather like a scarecrow and then would organize the games, stretched out on the grass, cheerful and charming as a prince who does as he wishes. The children, flattered by Jacques's involvement, meekly accepted his reprimands. The mood was peaceful; no one had any pity on Taneran; Jacques was king.

The mist, bitter and cold, enveloped everything now. Maud was quite sure that her younger brother was not fishing on the banks of the Dior; she felt the need, nevertheless, to go down to the edge of the stream. By hanging on to the acacia trunks in order to avoid sliding, she reached the railroad tracks. At the bottom of the hill on which the property was situated, a spring ran swiftly, surging up by leaps and bounds. As Maud crossed the field, the second train, whose whistle she could hear from Semoic onward, went by very quickly in the fog.

Then, in the jumble of reeds that bordered the banks, between the two mills of Semoic and Ostel, Maud perceived, as vague as a shadow, but nevertheless frighteningly precise, a woman's dead body floating by in the water. She cried out and instinctively ran back up the slope as quickly as she could.

Halfway up she stopped, suddenly clearheaded again, as if she felt abruptly outside of fear's bounds. Who was this woman . . . ? She hadn't recognized her face, having only seen her through the semidarkness. Clearly the stranger had died in the waters coming from the direction of the Semoic mill, alongside the fields that extended to the valley of the Uderan domain. This idea was suddenly unbearable, and she could not make up her mind to leave.

An instant later she realized that her cry had not been heard. A moment of reflection cautioned her not to notify anyone. What if she went to make sure the woman's floating body hadn't been stopped by the reeds in front of their property? And if it had been, what could Maud do? More than anything Maud had to see.

What was most difficult was to go back down the field she now crossed as calmly as if someone were watching her. Arriving at the embankment, she knelt on the ground in order to see as far as possible down the river.

Sometimes haltingly, sometimes moving with docility, the dead woman was being carried by the current. Maud followed her with her eyes until the floating body went beyond their fields and slowly penetrated into the alder woods that separated the Pecresse lands from their own. Just before the river's bend, by the day's last glimmer, Maud made out two black braids dragging along beside the corpse . . .

When she arrived at the road level, Maud saw a shape that made her step back: her mother! She felt acutely how much Mrs. Taneran, more sensitive and impressionable than her children, needed to be spared.

"I've been waiting and calling for quite a while. Where are you coming from?" The trembling voice of the older woman revealed her weakness.

"From the Dior, seeing if Henry wasn't there. He must be at Barque's."

"Mrs. Dedde invited both of us," added Mrs. Taneran. "I have to admit that it makes a nice change from the Pecresses."

Partially reassured, Maud's mother started off again on the conversation she had had with their neighbor the other night. "Believe it or not, that crazy Pecresse woman came to ask your hand in marriage for her son. The people around here don't suspect a thing! On top of that, she'd get a double deal. John is having an affair around here, the Deddes' daughter probably told you."

Maud was barely listening, not taking it in. The words whizzed by her ears, striking her head, which was already dizzy. She kept herself from showing the terrible revulsion she felt, not knowing its source.

"What's the matter, Maud? It's better than it was a while ago, my dear . . ." Her mother took her arm, but Maud shook it off in anger and walked more quickly. Mrs. Taneran followed her with sadness and repeated, without understanding the full scope of her words, "What holidays, my dear! We're two unhappy women, it seems, and sometimes I tell myself that if you weren't there it would be worse . . ."

When she was seated at the table in the bright light, Maud appeared overcome with fatigue, as if she had accomplished a task beyond her strength. In her weariness, everything became simpler. Her anxiety did not prevent her from chatting and eating heartily, though. Reassured, Mrs. Taneran entertained the tenant farmers.

At the end of the meal, someone knocked at the door. It was Alexis, Pellegrain's servant. He was returning from Semoic rather drunk and carrying a hurricane lamp. "It looks like Pecresse's lovebird has done herself in. You know who I mean, the one who was a waitress at Barque's?"

Maud didn't flinch. When Alexis had gone, Mrs. Dedde turned toward her. "Everyone knows that you've discouraged the young man's interest. Don't worry about it, Miss Grant. Anyway, he was waiting for an excuse to leave her. She was a poor young thing. Knowing Mrs. Pecresse, she'll be breathing more easily now!"

That evening, instead of returning to Uderan, Maud went to Barque's, as she had planned.

CHAPTER 8

THE BARQUE INN, NAMED FOR ITS NEW OWNER, WAS LOCATED in an old mill, just at the entrance to Semoic. The tall, dilapidated building had hardly changed since the mill had closed down. It was brightened up only by a small outside café overlooking the Dior, before the dam, at the widest part of the river. People came from The Pardal, Mirasmes, and Ostel to enjoy themselves in the evening; it was a way of getting fresh air and taking a walk along the Dior.

The main room was situated above the water, accessed by means of a little wooden bridge. Barque had decorated it in a country style: tables covered with heavy cotton cloths surrounded the tiled central area, where people occasionally danced. Across from the door that opened onto the balcony, a small modern counter in aluminum, with stools, made the place resemble the outdoor dancing cafés in Paris. Behind the counter stood Barque, still young, dressed in an impeccable short-sleeved shirt. He spent the three summer months in

Semoic for his health and then returned to Paris, where he had a bar.

From the road, Maud heard the cries of the rescue workers scouring the thickets and those of the rowers calling out to one another as they got closer in the fog. The scandal that kept everyone on the alert that evening seemed to her to be a good excuse for finding George again.

Behind closed doors, people were dancing at Barque's. A thick smoke in the room created a kind of anonymity. Among the dancers, she recognized her two brothers, and at a table opposite the entrance was George Durieux.

Leaning up against the wall, he looked at her as he smoked. His nervous gestures and the expression on his face indicated that he had trouble containing a joyous impatience. He gave the impression that he, too, had waited for her, without actually trying to see her again, for reasons still unknown to Maud. She had never understood it so clearly before this night.

As everyone was watching out for newcomers, the young woman's entrance was noticed, and Jacques cast an inquiring glance her way, which in times past would have made her shudder.

As soon as she saw Jacques, she noticed her brother's agitation. Neither women nor dancing could give him this look of living intensely in the moment. He resembled a wild animal that stalks the forest, incessantly on the lookout for danger. Whatever he was doing, the entrance door fascinated him; he continuously looked over at Barque with the naïve confidence of a fearful child.

The gramophone played without breaks, and the dancers hardly took time to rest in between dances. However, at the first break, Jacques and Henry came toward their sister, intrigued. "What's going on?"

"Nothing, I was getting bored, that's all."

Her brothers were not happy with this answer. Henry shrugged his shoulders and Jacques called to the bartender, in an embarrassed voice, "Are you going to take care of my sister, Barque?" For a moment people scrutinized her with curiosity and distrust. Barque brought her a glass of alcohol and without a word took up his place behind the counter again.

The atmosphere between the dances was strangely silent and not at all reassuring, as if the music covered up a general malaise. People danced, rested, and drank, carried along by a sort of rhythm as regular as that of gymnastics. Maud noticed that her older brother and George never spoke to each other.

Although younger than Jacques, George appeared to be his age. Jacques Grant had that look of apparent youth that one sees in losers, pleasure seekers, and those who have never had any real responsibility to cause them to age, or any habit to gentrify them. His passion for women incited him to pursue one affair after another and prevented him from getting stuck in any particular relationship.

Their age difference was felt even less because Durieux had experienced much in his life. He was neither proud nor cynical of the soft life he lived, whereas Jacques showed off his idleness in front of just about anyone. He claimed that he preferred not to devote himself to any of the many possibilities he saw for himself, for fear of upsetting others or putting them down. He liked feeling at each instant of his life that childlike illusion of still being able to undertake anything.

"I should write, but you see, when you write, you are half-done. You are diminished, worn-out, it's disgusting . . . and really, what for?" Perhaps it was not only laziness that put these words in Jacques Grant's mouth. The inanity of human existence had become an article of faith for him.

No doubt nothing significant had ever crossed George Durieux's path. He obviously suffered from that and had made a habit of entrenching himself, silently, behind his disappointment. He appeared to take so little interest in life and people that they thought him to be rich with dreams and gifted with a kind of inner contentment.

This evening, all of that revealed itself suddenly to Maud, even though she had thought for a long time that Durieux and Jacques were fundamentally similar.

Young women sat on the barstools. Henry probably knew them. He spoke to them with a great deal of familiarity, calling them by their first name and grabbing them by the waist. These were not the farm girls, but young women from Bordeaux who spent their holidays in the area. Even if Henry led a degenerate life, he inspired confidence and was likable. No constraints had built up his distrust or slowed down his winged race toward pleasure. One felt, even though he was young, that he already possessed a real experience of love; he loved chastely and with the tenderness of a child.

Jacques managed the whole scene, paying for the dances, requesting the musical numbers. At a certain point he came up to Henry and said something to him with an exasperated look, while pointing at Maud. But his younger brother shrugged his shoulders and kept on dancing.

Jacques then went up to the second floor by means of a small staircase that Maud had taken for a door hidden by the counter. It was Barque's apartment. People got together there in more intimate circles, either because they didn't want to dance or because the music prevented them from talking. Before going up, although he seemed to have shown no interest in Maud until then, he spoke to her sharply: "You'd better get going now, you hear? I paid for your drink . . ."

But she had no desire to leave or to obey him. The glass of alcohol that Barque had served her gave her a refreshing boldness. Her brother went away without insisting. People began to dance again in the smoke-filled semidarkness.

When George got up in turn, Maud thought he was getting ready to leave. Deciding to follow him and ignoring the awkwardness it could create, she made a move to get up. Perhaps he understood, but he didn't look as if he had noticed.

She told him she had come to see him. From time to time she had moments of incredible audacity. "Why, from one day to the next, did you stop coming? People just don't do that . . ."

He appeared to take her remark as one of those overblown social niceties people think it is proper to use. No, he didn't want to sit down. "I'll walk you home in a bit if you would like me to."

She saw by the look in his eyes that he was so troubled by a violent desire for her presence that he lost his normal composure and firmness. All of a sudden, a long habit of restraint exploded on his face: until now he had dominated it and had held himself, lightly and airily, at the summit of the powerful wave of his suppressed ardor. Maud understood that he was now letting himself be submerged by the very same defense he had imposed upon himself, was suddenly losing his sense of unreality, and was abandoning himself all at once to the deep and bitter wave of his desire. This appeared and vanished like a shock wave when they looked at each other, in the space of a second. George went back to his place. The instant left Maud with warm, bright glimmers inside. She had the feeling of being happy and believed that happiness was the prerogative of those magic moments when difficulties all disappear, even in the midst of the disorder created by a catastrophe.

In reality, he had thought less about Maud in the last while because a man, in order to remember, needs the beginning of a sense of possession, a commitment. While he had noticed her at the dinner at Uderan, this was also apparent to Jacques, who couldn't stand losing a friend. To distance her from George he had invented a story: "You didn't know that my sister was engaged to John Pecresse? They're getting married in the fall." (Jacques secretly wished it was true. Pecresse would have provided some revenue for the use of Uderan, which would have served Jacques well.)

It took a certain amount of time before Durieux stopped coming back to the domain. He eventually avoided taking the way through Uderan. The farmers confirmed what Jacques Grant had said. This marriage seemed odious to him; however, he stayed away because Maud didn't belong to him, by either a word or even a kiss.

Now that she was here, this evening, he felt liberated from the interdiction he had imposed on himself. And all of a sudden, he felt diabolically happy that this misunderstanding had occurred, because it gave an unexpected depth to his romantic venture.

Just when nobody expected it, John Pecresse entered the room. Barque quickly rushed over and stopped the gramophone. People came running, the women in front, with thoughtless cries.

"So, nothing?"

"My poor fellow, sit down . . ."

John Pecresse stared at them with a haggard look. "Nothing," he said.

On seeing Maud, he no doubt had the wrong idea as to her presence there and thought she was there for him . . . Leaving aside good manners, as is permitted in certain circumstances, he sat down across from her. He had the distorted face of someone who has just been shaken by fear (the most astonishing of fears, that of having caused a death).

Treacherously, the music covered up his entry, and people were dancing again. It must have been around midnight. George Durieux didn't budge, but only ordered a drink from time to time.

John Pecresse told Maud how happy he was to see her. It displeased the young woman that John had come to her table, benefiting distastefully from the situation—and all the more so because he was drinking a lot, with the alcohol acting quickly on his overextended nerves.

"You didn't know that she was a servant here? You wouldn't think so, would you, seeing people dance like that with no respect? I hadn't come here for a while; I have no idea what happened."

Maud thought about her brother's embarrassed look when she entered, the complicity of the whole room, and George's more or less obvious complicity . . . , but no, she believed that John Pecresse, frightened by the death of his mistress, sought to unload a heavy responsibility on someone else. "If I ask Jacques for explanations," continued the young man, "he'll jump on me. But we'll know the truth; I'll tell it to the whole region."

Pecresse drank coarsely, glass after glass, like a fellow from the countryside, licking his lips after each swig, calling to Barque continuously in an angry and vulgar voice. But no one provoked him, and people avoided speaking to him. Maud alone stayed near him, caught between the desire to keep him from speaking badly of her family and not wanting to miss George again.

"Why do you say that it's my brother who pushed her to the edge? It's cowardly not to recognize that you had dropped her a long time ago. If my brother got her a job here, it's to his credit."

"Did you hear that, Barque? It's to Monsieur Jacques's credit if he got rid of the girl for me! What family solidarity! To think that you probably didn't even pay her, you old bastard, Barque! Go on, give me a couple more, you owe it to me!" Barque complied right away, swiftly, determined to resist all the provocations.

Leaning toward Maud, John added, "What if we drank to our engagement? Don't you know that it's for the love of you that I dropped her?" He repeatedly got up and sat down clumsily. She noticed with relief that a number of clients were leaving. Barque behind his counter and George at the back of the room seemed not to notice anything. The music had stopped.

"You realize that if you refuse, it will go badly for you. Your mother has even borrowed the money for your brother's furniture from my mother. That's pride, all right! We know what you're worth around here . . ." Maud didn't know this detail, but it didn't surprise her.

John Pecresse collapsed, his head in his arms and breathing heavily. Maud barely had time to reflect on the young man's revelations. The sound of a voice could be heard on the second floor, and the door at the top of the stairway opened with a noise that, in comparison to the silence now reigning in the room, exploded like a thunderbolt. Barque rushed to warn Jacques. Pecresse woke up, crying out insults in a thick, menacing voice.

At that moment, George stood up facing the stairway and Maud placed herself in front of him, facing the stairs. Fearfully, the last guests grouped themselves behind the two of them. Maud saw her brother on the landing and understood that there were people begging him not to go down.

Maud realized that George stood behind her, ready to touch her, but she suddenly felt such a desire to see her brother come down that she was not moved. Was Jacques able to take off in front of Pecresse? She alone, over whom he had reigned for so many years as elder brother, as lord of the family, felt that she was able to reach him in his vanity. "I think it's time to go home, Jacques."

He replied in a loud, expressionless voice, "My sister is right, it's time to go home, my old Barque . . ."

Jacques came down and appeared so pale in the light that he

was unrecognizable. Slowly, he went up to Pecresse, gaining back his courage when he saw the young man was drunk. In a noble gesture, he put his hand on John's shoulder. "What's happened to you is terrible, John, and I truly understand your misfortune. See what it is to encourage a woman? Your anger doesn't make any sense, Pecresse. You know I did everything to help her out. Remember what you told me a couple of weeks ago. I'm a good man, you know it yourself. We've known each other for fifteen years . . ."

The iron fist that clasped his shoulder prevented Pecresse from getting up. With a wavering hand he seemed to dodge Jacques Grant's words, but he didn't say anything back. Jacques took advantage of the situation with admirable composure and skill. "Come on, let's drink a glass together to forget this nasty affair! Maud, come and drink with us! Don't worry, Pecresse, I know your thoughts about my sister, and I can help you out more than you think." Nobody came to sit at their table. The clients surrounded and encouraged Pecresse, who continued to drink.

As Maud was about to leave, a clamor was heard outside and some men came in. One of them went toward the miller and took off his cap. The man was perspiring heavily, his put-tees wet and his uniform damp. It was one of the search-and-rescue workers. He glanced at the onlookers with a certain disdain and spoke to Barque. "We found her past the woods, in front of the Pecresses' field, caught in the reeds at the bend in the Dior where there's no current."

In a flash, Pecresse and Jacques Grant were on their feet. Pecresse looked at the rescue workers, one after the other. He hopped oddly from one foot to the other, and finally broke

down in tears, repeating with a dull voice and such shameless-
ness that no one pitied him, "At the same place where we met
for four years, following my military service . . ."

Soon other search-and-rescue farmers entered. They didn't
deign to answer the patrons' questions. The only one they
knew was Pecresse. To him they explained, "We left her on
the riverbank. Tomorrow the mayor will come and make the
official report. There's no reason, because she was alone . . ."

Maud thought she had been seen in the field by the Dior,
but it soon became obvious: no one was looking at her and
the farmers' words were not at all ambiguous. She regained
her calm, a calm that prevented her from feeling the least bit
of emotion. She finally dared to look at her brother; he was
leaving his friends. A look of satisfaction, discreet but obvious, showed on his face.

The Barque Inn closed up. Maud found herself alone on the
road while the night was still pitch-black, having left before
everyone else.

The more she tried to put together the drama of the
night, the more she was afraid of her brother's attitude,
which appeared cowardly and intense at the same time. How
strangely conciliatory he had shown himself to be! The face
he was wearing as he came down the stairs kept passing before
her eyes, both mocking and terrified, although she could not
grasp the meaning of it.

Hadn't she just helped Jacques out without knowing it, by
not revealing that the young woman had certainly not committed suicide in front of the Pecresse place? She didn't regret
having encouraged her brother in that way to confront John,

but she understood at the same time that she would have no rest before having some kind of certainty about the reasons for the young woman's demise. Maud sank into senseless hypotheses, and sometimes her doubts carried her quite far; evil took on a form so far removed from anything she had known until now that she could hardly stand its view.

It was at the crossroads of the highway to Bordeaux and the road to Semoic that George caught up with her. She was neither happy nor surprised. George confronted her abruptly. "What John Pecresse said was true; your brother made life impossible for that poor girl. He began to hate her after shamelessly possessing her; I know too much now to keep quiet. There are things that are appalling even if they don't affect one directly. I did everything I could to keep him from acting the way he did, out of respect for you and your mother, but Jacques is a nasty fellow . . ."

Maud was not ignorant of the kind of torture Jacques could inflict on a woman who had begun to displease him. However, she wondered why George had wanted to be there that evening, knowing the circumstances. Instinctively, she tried again to defend her brother.

"Why do you attack Jacques? I thought you were his friend. Furthermore, if he were as guilty as you say he is, he would not have gone up to Pecresse so confidently, earlier on."

George's voice quickly lost its habitual indifference. It took on a tone that Maud did not recognize, expressing his anger laden with hurt. "Jacques wasn't proud; you know it yourself, Maud. The young woman was also involved with Barque, whose child she was expecting. She was never paid, and your brother figured out a way to push her over the edge . . . I don't deny that John Pecresse had a lousy role in it, far from that. But I've known John for a long time. He would never have made her suffer like that—he doesn't have Jacques's ingenuity and temperament . . ."

Maud wanted George to stop talking about her brother.

"Moreover, you better be careful yourself, Maud," he continued. "God knows what Jacques will come up with to gain Pecresse's confidence back! I don't know you well, but when I saw you encouraging your brother this evening, I saw how important he is to you, and how your family is united around him."

George wanted to go back to Uderan with Maud. He was now speaking without her encouraging him, either by word or by action.

Once they were in the dining room at Uderan, there was a long stretch of silence before she knew what to say to him. She had the impression he was there on account of weakness, so he wouldn't have to go home alone after this night. She had waited for this moment for so long but didn't feel any happiness in being with him, as if from now on it was too late to continue loving each other. She thought once again that she didn't feel anything for George and that everything was destroyed: her illusions, her will to be happy, her strength, without her knowing why.

George was smoking, leaning up against the chimney and speaking to Maud from time to time, continuing to clarify his thoughts. They both put on formal airs; despite themselves, they took on the embarrassed, somber look of people who find themselves caught in misfortune.

Maud believed that the time to admit what she knew would

not come again. She had to tell George now. Such an unexpected confidence would create a shock and break the bad spell that had been over them this night, and would perhaps bring him back.

She murmured, "Last night, after the storm, I discovered her in front of our field, below the railroad tracks. I'm sure she drowned there. I suppose it would have been possible to think she had ended up there, but it would have been unlikely after coming from the mill."

George did not reply right away. "It doesn't surprise me that you kept silent. You won't always be able to keep him out of trouble, fortunately . . ."

She had thought that George would judge her to have self-esteem and was vexed. Now the unbelievable moment of his departure was approaching, and even if she knew she had charm, she felt she no longer had the means to hold on to him . . .

Suddenly someone knocked several times on the shutter. A moment went by and the muffled, oppressed voice of Jacques Grant could be heard. "Maud, open up!" The voice was pleading, with childlike gentleness.

Maud stepped toward the door. George held her back and covered her mouth with his hand to prevent her from responding. They waited for a moment like that, and, even though it was no longer necessary, George didn't let go; tears dropped onto his hand and he drew Maud close, holding her tight against him. The young woman understood that he felt the same deliverance that she did: together they came out of a dark and difficult night.

George leaned over and said very quietly, "I've loved you

for a long time, Maud. Can you believe that Jacques claimed you were engaged to Pecresse? That's why I fled . . ."

Jacques walked around the house. They heard him knocking on the shutters of the bedrooms, discreetly, without impatience. Coming back to the dining room, he began to call his sister again. While still speaking in a low voice, he wrote something against the shutter. For a moment, the scratching of a pencil broke the silence; then Jacques slid a note into the crack of the door and walked away.

They rushed to get it, and Maud read aloud from her brother's small and almost undecipherable writing: "My dear Maud, I advise you to keep to yourself everything you have seen and heard tonight. You are old enough to understand that our mother must know nothing about this.—Jacques."

George said in a softened tone, "I know he loves your mother deeply, in his own way . . ." He was struck by the exultant expression on the young woman's face when she responded.

"We all love Jacques, as extraordinary as that may seem, even Taneran, his first victim. Although Jacques makes people unhappy, he also manages to suffer for it sometimes and regret not being better. He'll probably walk around all night like a madman; he came to talk to me. When he's like that, he's afraid of himself."

For an instant she had the desire to call out to her brother, but George held her back.

CHAPTER 9

AS THEY HAD IN THE PAST, THE TANERANS SPENT THEIR SUN-days at the place of an old friend, Mr. Briol, a retired teacher who lived in The Pardal. That morning, for the fourth time since their arrival, they crossed their large property.

In the Sunday calm, one could barely hear the Riotor bab-bling below the plateau, reduced as it was to a tiny stream in the wake of the big drought that had followed the week of the storm. The Tanerans set out through the old prune orchards, and the vines, caught up in a sort of vegetal madness, sent out long shoots on every side.

Before crossing the oak woods that stretched out at the end of their property on the south, they went alongside the estate's tenant farmhouse. The Dedde girl was standing in the doorway, ready to leave for mass. She fidgeted and smiled at Henry in a way that expressed so vulgarly a recent involve-ment that the youngest of the Tanerans turned his head away.

When they were on the road, he used the pretext of a flock of birds flying high in the sunlit sky to hide his embarrass-ment. "Look, Maud!" In the dark, slanted eyes of her young brother, Maud saw the shadow of the wood pigeons reflected. His head back, he followed their flight until the moment when it blended into the azure sky.

When they got to the rocky road that wound through the vineyards, Mrs. Taneran had difficulty going forward. She had gained some weight during her leisurely holidays, and, despite the morning freshness, she felt tired and out of breath. "I'm not used to doing anything anymore. I'm getting heavy," she moaned, wiping her forehead.

Her plaintive tone garnered no sympathy from any of her children. Her sons walked in front of her. Henry sauntered from one side of the path to the other, like a young boy. Jacques, already tired of the pleasures of the country, stopped now and then to get his mother going again with the impatient call, "Well, are you coming?"

The moment he felt an insult bubbling up in him, it came out of his mouth. That was his way of being honest. And if he detested Maud's approach to things, it was precisely because she never expressed her feelings as spontaneously as he did. He never knew what effect his insults or attitude had on his sister, for his reproaches disappeared inside her in a mysterious murkiness, like a lake without currents. His mother always said of her son that as long as he was candid, he wasn't as bad as people claimed him to be. No doubt it was true, to the degree to which Jacques was not any harder than he appeared.

He had just received a long letter from the Tavares Bank, which he had refused to show to his mother. He said he was very worried and spoke about going back home. Could one read into that a pretext for leaving Uderan, where he had been more or less cast aside for the last while?

Since the waitress's suicide, Maud saw Jacques only at meals. He never spoke to her anymore. He was probably not unaware of the fact that George spent his evenings with his sister. At Barque's, he missed this friend who had slipped away from him and was secretly humiliated by it. Maud guessed that Jacques didn't have much fun anymore at Semoic and that a shameful feeling of distress had been torturing him since this affair. She knew through the Deddes' daughter that fewer people than before came to the inn.

Without admitting it to himself, Jacques feared his sister because he suspected her to be his most indomitable enemy. He wasn't sure that she would refrain from revealing anything to their mother if he dared to reproach her for monopolizing George Durieux, and all the more so because Jacques wasn't sure if his sister was George's mistress.

In the soft Sunday morning light, his mother considered her son with a sad tenderness, and one could guess by her look that she asked herself endless, tormenting questions about him. For the first time she doubted that he still wanted to settle down at Uderan, and she admitted it to him. She could be incredibly tactless at times, as she knew, but she could not hold her tongue, believing that it was her motherly duty to question him.

"In the beginning, we'll help you," she told him gently. "I'm sure that Taneran will help you. I can guarantee that this old estate is worth something these days . . ." Encouraged by his silence, she continued. "You'll come to see that I did well not to have sold it. I would like you to reassure me, Jacques. I have already incurred tremendous expense to set you up here."

Scornfully, he yelled at her to "keep Uderan" if she wanted to die there, but in that case, he would look for something else. An ugly discussion sprang up but soon ended, for both of them judged it useless to go any deeper. By her senseless devotion, Mrs. Taneran destroyed any desire her son might have had to escape. Her constant fervor irritated Jacques. One would have said, at times, that he reproached his mother for her very tenderness, realizing that her accommodating ways were making him grow softer. Nevertheless, he did not leave his family, because the blowups, as scandalous as they may have been, between Mrs. Taneran and her son, did not indicate anything more than the state of their nerves.

Mrs. Taneran and her children took a shortcut through the Pellegrains' property. Mrs. Pellegrain, who was watching out for them, came and joined them. She was Mrs. Pecresse's first cousin. Her Sunday "transformation" was to wear a bright-colored bonnet whose color contrasted with her scarlet complexion and wrinkled features, giving her a questionable look of extended youth and making this farm woman look like a lady of the night. They exchanged a few words.

"And your brother? Still doing well?" Mrs. Taneran inquired. Mrs. Pellegrain's brother was a deaf-mute she had agreed to take in, despite the natural aversion she had for this unfortunate man. He was reputed, though, to be the best worker in the region. He was known to be capable of doing the work of two men, which is why his brother-in-law never failed to hire him. Even if Mrs. Pellegrain did her best to show her affection for her brother, everyone in the village was aware that he never ate at the family table and slept in a closet under the stairs.

Maud tried to move away from her mother chatting with the farm woman, but the latter addressed Maud in a strong southern accent. "So, miss, it's nice to sleep at Uderan?" Maud felt herself reddening as if under the lash of a whip but responded boldly that, indeed, she enjoyed staying at the domain. She noticed that Jacques had stopped and was watching her in a half-mocking, disdainful way.

The deaf man came up to them, dressed in the clean, collarless shirt his sister made him wear on Sundays. When he saw the Tanerans, a big smile covered his face and curled his lips up over his enormous teeth. A sad, smothered sound came from his throat, expressing, no doubt, his contentment. But he didn't stop and quickly walked away with his mouth open.

They passed by the Big Oak Farm and then arrived at The Pardal. Although the village was much farther away from Uderan than Semoic, the Tanerans had the habit of going to mass at The Pardal because of the parish priest, whom they knew. During the service, Maud noticed that her brothers were as furious as they were embarrassed to have been led to such a place. Sunday invariably ended in dispute; Jacques and Henry saw that by attending mass they always fell into the trap their mother succeeded in laying for them. Already, young Henry used the same arguments as his older brother in accusing his mother of tricking them into another dreadfully boring Sunday. This insignificant detail perfectly illustrated one of the family's character traits: an incredible ability to forget! Indeed, what were they expecting and why did they have any illusions as to the day's unchanging flow? They betrayed in that way their incurable weakness. They had barely started out for The Pardal when they suddenly seemed to recall the boredom they would encounter. Yet they never turned around and, out of spite, contrived to make the day as infernal as possible. Still, they knew how to preserve a certain dignity, for they were as cowardly in regard to scandal as they were daring in front of their subdued mother. Thus, during the service, they sat in the first row of the chancel with a slightly humble and contented look, in order to honor the confidence of the Pardalians, who gave them the best place in the church. The village folk moved back even farther behind them, it seemed, to acknowledge the Tanerans' social standing.

As for Mrs. Taneran, she prayed only at intervals, letting herself be easily distracted by the people she recognized and at whom she smiled. The day's outlook didn't bother her at all.

Maud once again gauged the difference between this woman, with her rested and distracted look, and the overburdened creature whom their mother would become upon their return, when her sons would load her down like a donkey with the weight of their ill mood. Mrs. Taneran possessed an amazing energy that she saved up during these brief moments of profound diversion. Grace resulted from the habit of an existence whose blows she evaded daily.

All the farmers of The Pardal attended high mass. The women, to the right of the chancel, were mainly dressed in black sateen, which stretched out over their rounded backs, curved by their hard labor; the men, to the left, were fewer in number. Although the weather was beautiful outside, the sun filtered in faintly through the stained-glass windows. The choir sang around an old harmonium set up on the podium. The mother of the priest, the seamstress who had worked in

The Pardal for twenty years, and the latest member, the kindergarten assistant, composed The Pardal's choir.

Maud thought about George Durieux. Since the event at Barque's, he came to Uderan secretly every evening. They met in the dining room, behind closed doors. She had difficulty accepting the fear George felt for her brother. At the same time, she had just as much difficulty understanding George's attitude toward her. She would have preferred to see him as she imagined him, violent and unscrupulous and taking over her brother's role in dominating her life. It was her first love, and she didn't doubt that it would be the only one, as she could not do without the presence of this man. However, when he spoke to her about marriage, she found the idea to be naïve. Something in George seemed unassailable to her, and that was a faith in her that he had created on his own and for which she found no basis; this lack of judgment shocked her and made her impatient at the same time.

The house belonging to Mr. Briol, the retired schoolteacher, was on a series of terraces, with the church occupying the lowest one and the presbytery the highest. The reinforced terrace, transformed into a vegetable garden, was the continuation of an abandoned cemetery, which made up the base. From there, the view stretched out quite far, for the landscape descended in a gentle incline not impeded by any obstacle, except, in the middle, a little river lined with elm trees. Crossing the slope was a very white road, hidden in part by the landmass of The Pardal.

In the sheltered garden, with no shade, it was very hot. While Henry and Jacques went back and forth on the little wall-walk along the terrace, Mrs. Taneran and Maud leaned on the small wall that overlooked the valley. When Jacques arrived at the level of his mother, he declared through clenched teeth, "It's the last time, do you hear, the last time!"

Mrs. Taneran didn't reply. She only tried to appease him with a forced smile. The poor woman had never noticed how this exasperated her son even more. Maud, whose eyes were somewhat blinded by the midday sun, appeared anxious. Why did her brother's words permeate her in such a way? He paced the road nervously, like an animal in a cage that couldn't find a way out.

Even more than the other night, she formed a brutal inner judgment of Jacques, which would have dismayed him if he had guessed it. He believed himself to be, in fact, the nicest of men, the worthiest of the responsibilities of his family. Never before had Maud calculated so precisely the degree of contempt that he merited. Since she had come to know George Durieux, she was able to grasp the underlying temperament of her brother, first because she and George often talked about it, and then because it presently seemed of little consequence for Jacques to be contemptible or not. Her love for George freed her mind from a last, fragile obligation, and she now held the key to this mystery.

She finally understood the nature of what she had vaguely endured as an indisputable reality. This victory of enlightenment intoxicated her. Overwhelming arguments formed in her mind, and she thought she would share them with George that very evening, and that his love for her would gain some new depth, some new perversity, by welcoming such revelations . . .

Anger made her temples throb, but she managed to retain her joyous enthusiasm. All of a sudden, the strength she felt made her take pity on her mother, who was still suffering as blindly as ever under a tyranny that should have been so easy to cast off. Maud put her hand on her mother's hand. Mrs. Taneran did not understand the exact meaning of this gesture, but having turned around, she met her daughter's eyes and withdrew her hand . . .

The schoolteacher's sister arrived. Almost blind, she walked with a heavy step, and in the daylight her clothing looked disgustingly dirty. In each wrinkle of her elderly face was etched a fine black furrow that made it look deeper. "You're looking at the garden?" she said. "Oh, it's gotten very unruly since the lad died! Since the fall I haven't touched it . . ." The lad was their younger brother, also a teacher in a nearby village, who had passed away the previous year.

The woman looked annoyed. Every Sunday the Tanerans' visit caused her extra work. The only one to understand, much later, was Maud: the old woman would have preferred not to see them, because Mrs. Taneran's impetuosity and solicitude had never pleased her. She preferred Henry, who as a child had come to take Latin lessons from her son.

Mr. Briol had aged. He came in singing and went courteously toward his mother to encourage her. The good woman muttered something and then they all sat down at the table. Dinner was gloomy. Usually they didn't sit in the dining room, where the furniture seemed to be covered in a thin, gauzelike veil of dust. Flies, intoxicated by the sun, rushed violently toward the ceiling . . .

Her eyes glazed over, Maud stared at the garden without

seeing it, as birds flew over in joyful throngs, while Mrs. Taneran spoke intermittently. At a certain point, old Mr. Briol tried to amuse Henry with memories they had in common, but the teacher quickly understood that whatever had amused his student in the past didn't grab his attention anymore. Henry, like Jacques, had become indifferent to anything that didn't serve his pleasure.

After vespers the Tanerans went home tired. The day was ending. As soon as The Pardal disappeared, Mrs. Taneran said, to avoid repeating the same old scene, "I think that if all goes well, we'll leave by the end of the week . . ."

They remained silent. She had just expressed the resolution her sons vaguely hoped for. Nothing, at present, nothing could have kept them at Uderan. Maud felt invaded by a bitterness that was mitigated, it was true, by a feeling of detachment so immense that she felt she had never loved them.

The road stretched out under their feet. The silent form of Uderan appeared. They walked around it and headed toward the hostile home of Mrs. Pecresse.

CHAPTER 10

AT DINNER THAT NIGHT, MRS. TANERAN ANNOUNCED HER departure with such insistence that it seemed almost inappropriate. Mrs. Pecresse wasn't expecting it and immediately envisioned the catastrophe that was about to descend upon her family. Once Maud was gone, what would happen to her son? Not only did Maud avoid him, but since the suicide of his girlfriend, John was looked upon in The Pardal as a dishonest young man to whom people would hesitate to give their daughter in marriage.

In the mind of the Pecresse woman, it was because of his love for Maud that John had given up his mistress. She didn't know that Jacques, in turn, had abandoned and mistreated the young woman. Mrs. Pecresse continued to cling to the first part of the story, believing in her son's guilt. Happily for the Tanerans, she went about moping with disappointment and made no effort to find out the truth.

Mrs. Pecresse knew about her son's weakness, like her own, for stubbornly insisting on getting what he wanted. Thus, since that tragic night, she feared the worst—for example, that John would leave her. The disdain her son had shown her in the last little while was as terrible for the Pecresse woman as the thought of her own death. Wasn't the only way of fixing things up to keep Maud at Uderan? Even if Miss Grant turned out to be a young woman whose reputation was no longer intact, even if she had become of late the object of public scandal, she certainly remained desirable, and John did not stop wanting her even more than before.

However, during the dinner, the Pecresse woman did not show her concern in the least. She did her best to appear friendly and to cause the faults she found in the Tanerans to be forgotten. Completely focused on her own designs, she didn't stop to ask herself whether her plans compromised the very existence of the Taneran family, which already appeared so disunited. But even if she had realized, she would not have hesitated to move ahead, because her behavior was completely dictated by her passions.

That night, Maud Grant left very early for Uderan. She headed straight for the loquat hedge, where weeks earlier she had turned away John Pecresse. There, she stopped a moment to catch her breath. It was light outside, even though the moon hadn't yet risen. On her right, in the Dior valley, the mist was gathering with the weightlessness of foam. On the other side of the path, the Uderan plateau stretched out as far as the eye could see, bare and motionless.

What a despicable Sunday! From the morning onward something had been hovering over them—their final determination to leave Uderan. Concluding such a day couldn't have been any different. After that, how light they had felt in returning to the Pecresses'!

As soon as she was alone, however, Maud felt as awake as if she had been sleeping all day. All of a sudden, Sunday was far behind her, and she inhaled the perfume of her regained solitude, which blended with the pungent fragrance of the night. "What an awful day! How they disgust me," she repeated to herself. "They would disgust anyone . . ."

But she was already mulling over her words without feeling their reality. Indeed, she was getting closer to George, whom she was dying to see. The young man was supposed to be waiting for her at Uderan, under the linden trees. He would be coming on foot, no doubt, and would be smoking while waiting for her. Under the trees she would be able to discern him only by the light of his cigarette. He would be nervous and ill-disposed, but she was glad, because he concealed his real self less and less with her. She set out again quickly, fearing he might leave before she got back to Uderan.

There was no one under the linden trees, and no noise, except that of the wind in the pine trees, rough and monotonous, like the sound of the sea on the beach pebbles. No matter how much she searched, there was no one.

She went into her room, not knowing what to do, and finally sat down near the pedestal table. "He should come, all the same, at this time . . ." From the top of the road she would hear him. Even before hearing him, she would discern the sound of his steps, she thought.

Almost immediately, her impatience knew no bounds. Would he come on foot or on horseback? The sound of galloping seemed to come from everywhere at once, tiring her mind and throwing her off center. The man was coming from every direction, from all the roads filled with night, and she didn't know where to place her hope. How tormenting was this multiple approach, which closed in on her as if she were in the middle of a circle that grew ever tighter and menacing!

Didn't he usually come earlier? My God, what did this mean? In thinking about their encounter the night before, she thought he must be suffering from the strictness he so naïvely imposed upon himself. "If you don't mind," he had said, "I won't keep coming as often; it's difficult, given the conditions in which we're seeing each other . . . I think it would be more fitting on my part to speak to your mother . . ."

She had laughed at the obstacles that he himself created, observing with satisfaction how much the temptation to go further tortured him more and more each day.

Even though she was breathing deeply, the air she took in got lost in her body as if through a leak at the bottom of her lungs, making her suffocate. She looked intensely through the barred window, scrutinizing the path through the linden trees, where gusts of wind were stirring up the leaves. "He's having fun making me wait. I know him . . ."

She spoke out loud, no longer able to overcome her impatience. The sound of her voice surprised her, and it seemed as if everything around her sent it back in successive echoes. "He's having fun; he's having fun making me wait; I know him; he's having fun . . ."

There were a hundred ways to understand it. He was having fun. He was having fun, no doubt a bit brutally, like the children of the region who pluck fish from under the rocks, barefoot in the torrents (maybe he was in the greenhouse, watching her). Perhaps he was also playing the odious game of the man who heightens his pleasure through an exasperating wait.

At this thought, her impatience became frenzied. Her attraction to George had grown as he had made himself scarcer these last few days. She got up, turned off the light, and went out.

The moon had now risen, and Maud's hunched-up shadow danced beside her like a little animal, happy to follow her. On the plateau, the wind was barely blowing, and the smell of hay floated over the pasturelands of the Dior. There was still nobody on the roads.

Maud walked very quickly. Her freedom intoxicated her, all the more so because it was only an apparent freedom. Her own folly amused her. How surprised he would be to see her! She was going to trap him, and he couldn't escape back to his own place, the way he fled Uderan every night.

She turned off toward the village. Only a few windows were still lit up, the blinds closed; the labored breathing coming from a few houses was evidence of the torpidity of this summer night. Maud moved away from the inhabited areas and went by an abandoned building—the home of a man who had hanged himself. The tragic event had taken place shortly after they had moved into Uderan; she remembered it well. Fear seized her, as it always did in going past the house, but a force stronger than fear compelled her to go on.

When she reached the lane lined with cypress trees she stopped. The house was lit up; she was no longer in danger of missing George. She felt a bit of shame in coming here. Her heart was beating so wildly she could hardly stand the pounding in her temples and throughout her whole body.

For a moment, the image of her mother sleeping in the large guest room at the Pecresses' passed before her eyes.

Maud feared the moment she was in and also loathed the idea that she was hiding herself.

Tomorrow—what would tomorrow be like if her mother learned something? Standing still, she tried to bring back the image of her mother in a fit of rage, terrible and ugly. But her attempt to scare herself was in vain. Her mother was still sleeping with the humble and tired face of a vanquished woman, and Maud could not picture her in the heat of anger or an emotional outbreak. "She'll never know I came; how would she know? That's the only thing that counts . . ."

She thought about her brothers, who, like her, "ran around." Taneran was right—she felt like them. This resemblance that she had vaguely foreseen up until now was reinforced today. She believed she was no longer bringing her love to George, but avowing a base and shameful sentiment.

The landscape stretched out before her, vast and unclouded, and nothing could stop her from continuing on. Her enormous freedom remained as an invitation. Moreover, for the last while she'd noticed that all potential barriers came tumbling down as she approached them. Even Jacques did not dare do anything against her, and didn't she hold George in her power?

At the stomping of the horse in the yard, she realized that George was about to go out. She bumped gently into the door panel as she slid the palm of her hand over the rough door. A footstep could be heard in the room and George appeared. "You were going down to Semoic?" she inquired.

"No, I was just getting ready to come and see you. How did you . . ."

She didn't answer and he immediately understood the

reason for her late-night escapade. Her goal achieved, she lost interest in what would follow. She headed to the back of the room, near the empty fireplace. On a little table, a lamp was burning low. She looked all around her like someone who doesn't recognize anything and wants to escape. At that point he took her lightly by the arm and pushed her back onto an easy chair. She allowed him to do it without saying anything, then once again scrutinized the apartment.

At her right stood a narrow couch with a broken edge on which some old, dog-eared books, clearly read more than once, had slipped from a bookcase. A stairway went up from the room itself, as in English country homes, and part of the ceiling, lower than the rest, must have represented the bedroom. A few dissimilar but good-quality pieces of furniture gave the place a surprising look of luxury, although each piece seemed to have been chosen for its own beauty and not in relation to the whole.

George was leaning against the entrance door. He didn't speak but contemplated this young girl who came to him so naturally, as if he had transported her with his gaze. The light of the lamp grew brighter. His shirt was partly open; he was breathing irregularly as he forced himself to keep calm. His dark eyes, fairly close together, and his broad forehead gave his face a determined look. "I'll bring in the horse and then I'll be right back," he said at last.

She said sweetly that he shouldn't go out of his way for her. She understood from his look that he was giving her time to get away if she wanted to. But as soon as he went out, she was seized with the same impatience to see him as before. The horse went by close to the wall. There was a moment of profound silence, during which she wrung her hands with irritation while repeating in a tortured voice, "What can he be doing? What on earth can he be doing?"

When he came back, she calmed down right away. He sat on the couch with his hands behind him; she sensed he was still giving her the freedom to decide on their fate, and this extreme sensitivity annoyed her.

"I came because I've had enough," she said suddenly. "Again today, they've been unbearable."

"I realize that," he replied.

"We're leaving next week—did you know that?" she added.

He didn't flinch. Next week? He suddenly felt the strength to change the course of events . . . "I doubt it," he muttered. She eyed him suspiciously.

"That poor schoolteacher Briol," Maud continued. "If you had seen the trouble he goes to in order to entertain my family . . . it was painful. What's extraordinary is that people bend over backward to please them, while . . ." Whenever she talked about her family, she always let herself get caught up in her own words. "While in fact they don't count, they're nobodies, you know, what people call nobodies . . ." She punctuated her comments with excessive gestures. He wasn't surprised that she had come so far to tell him things like that.

At Uderan, too, the two of them hadn't stopped talking about Jacques since the affair with the young waitress, but tonight it seemed as if she kept repeating a lesson poorly learned. (Even though they were upset with Jacques, they didn't betray him and stood by passively when the Pecresses were unjustly criticized in town.) "Quiet, my dear. Calm down," said George.

As soon as he came in, she had understood. George's irritation, his persistence in always wanting to leave her, had mysteriously stopped. A storm had passed over this man, but now he was there before her, perfectly calm. With short sentences he tried to calm her, even though he didn't believe she was truly angry.

He had struggled in order not to come to this point, but from the moment he felt vanquished, he was grateful for her victory, yielding to a gentleness full of abandon and appreciation; it showed as much in his eyes as in his drained voice, in his closed hands. "I wasn't expecting you," said George. "Every evening, and from morning onward, I wait patiently for the time to come and see you."

The familiar tone of his voice drew her closer to him. From now on they understood each other totally—from the simple beginning of their gestures, which became unnecessary to complete, to their most banal words, which they no longer deemed necessary to finish. An adorably full silence began to be possible. They had ceased being two.

All at once he got up. She guessed he was going to approach her. As short as this instant was, she could not stand the imminence of his approach. For a second, as she returned to an individual state again, her modesty reappeared intact, along with a self-defensive instinct that frightened her. She closed her eyes. She just had the time to hear herself pleading inwardly with herself to be weak, and very quickly gave in to this voice, succeeding in detaching herself from her will, like a leaf in the wind being torn away from the tree and allowing itself to be carried off, accomplishing finally its desire to die.

•   •   •

When she woke up, a bit of daylight had begun, laboriously, to show. It was true, they had forgotten to close the shutters.

She remained completely motionless for a time, unable to make a move. Between the sheets she felt her naked body, which she was no longer ashamed of, and which became a living form, like her face. In the past, she had used her body to counter unhappiness, requiring it, for example, to carry her out of the house, to laugh, to console her, or to weep comforting tears . . .

However, this particular morning, her body stayed in total harmony with her spirit, inert. Nothing was making an effort in this complicity and she thought very calmly of violent things.

George slept beside her; hair sprung from his bare arms, which he had wrapped around his head. He was handsome, as such, and the forearms of his tanned skin were marked by sunburns and all the traces and scars left behind by swimming, hunting, and other adventures. His sleep was childlike—confident and peaceful.

He appeared to Maud full of both strength and innocence. He had resisted, and now he rested, with abandon, at her side.

How would they see each other after this encounter? She avoided touching him; she watched him sleep. Yet she felt the need to roll up against him and go back to sleep, to gradually lose consciousness again beside him, on condition that he didn't move or ask her any questions.

She couldn't resist putting out her hand and stroking his shoulder, perhaps to bring him back a bit into reality. But instead she drifted off again into her dreams; he didn't move.

Did he still love her? She kept herself at the surface of her sleep, light and annoying, like an irritating fly. He sensed that she was there, at his side, for he grunted and murmured something incomprehensible and sank into sleep once again. What brought her suffering, she would have to endure alone.

It was now almost day. She arose and got dressed. Once she had made this first effort, she was in a hurry to get it over with. She had no trouble letting herself out, for everything had been left open in the rush of the night before. The road seemed long, she was shivering, and a stabbing pain in her lower body prevented her from running.

As she left the cypress lane, she looked back and considered George's home, drab in the early morning. Was she dreaming? She thought she saw a human form briskly leave the road. She pushed aside the suspicion that came to her, as she would have done a bad omen one conjures up without thinking about it again. When she caught sight of Uderan, she could not repress a strange smile.

In the mirror she noticed her pale coloring and haggard eyes. Once undressed, her naked body took on a beauty of which she had just become conscious and that left her both sad and proud. George had said so much about it to her, and his sentences came back to her in fragments. She tried in vain to bring them back in their warmth and spontaneity.

She had a hard time putting her ideas together. Soon she wasn't thinking of anything, except her mother, who might come to Uderan at any moment. She remained, however, unperturbed. "Bah! It's just foolishness, all that, just foolishness . . ."

A pain rose from her lower parts, warmly emanating like the memory of her pleasure. She buried herself in the freezing-cold sheets and quickly succumbed to a vertiginous sleep that left her without dreams.

CHAPTER 11

MAUD DID NOT GO BACK TO THE PECRESSE HOME UNTIL EVE-
ning, after roaming all day down by the Riotor. As soon as
she entered, she realized that no one in the room was speaking. It seemed that nobody noticed her presence and that they
were all preoccupied by the same concern. Even Mr. Pecresse,
after pulling up a chair for her, returned to his motionless
position by the fireplace, between his dogs.

Mrs. Taneran wasn't there. Maud was struck by the absence
of her mother, for the usual time for dinner had gone by without anyone paying any heed. A kind of suppressed fear rose
in Maud. What did she come looking for at the Pecresses?
Shouldn't she have stayed at George Durieux's place instead
of fleeing in the morning? She sat down, seemingly calm.

From time to time the two griffons lying near the fireplace vigorously scratched their sides; Maud remembered that
the odor of racing dogs sickened her mother, who invariably
asked, every evening, that they open the windows a little.
(This evening the windows were closed, in the absence of
their mother.)

Through the windows one could see the Dior in the distance, smoking like a brush fire and spreading a refreshing humidity, as if it had exhaled, with the coming of evening, a vapor carefully contained during the day. Sitting beside the window, the Pecresse son was looking at the view without really seeing it, while continuously redirecting his gaze toward Maud, to show her that her indifference tortured him.

Jacques and Henry, sitting close enough to touch each other, remained idle. After a moment, Maud went up to her younger brother: "What's going on? Can you tell me where Mother is?"

Henry gave her an angry look, stiffened his mouth in an expression of forced indignation, while Jacques appeared to be waiting for his sister to come to him. In Jacques's hollow cheeks his muscles played, round and hard like marbles. His lips were pale from being stretched over his teeth, and a blank stare, characteristic of his bad times, filtered through his half-closed eyes.

The Pecresse woman was exultant. By her look, by her sinuous walk through the room, one could make out an expression of satisfaction that she could barely keep inside. She, at least, found herself at home in this room where a dismal silence persisted. With a light step she went from one to the other, engaging them. Her southern accent, usually so unpleasant, softened and gave her voice an unexpected sweetness.

She flattered them with her gestures, her looks. One minute she spoke to her son: "John, dear, if you would like to smile a bit you would make your mother happy." The next moment she spoke to Henry Taneran: "Pick up the newspaper and let us know what's going on. My poor son, John, won't be the one to do that right now. Ah! John. Ah! John . . ." No one deigned to reply because, in spite of it all, her pretense did not escape them, and it revolted them.

Maud scrutinized them all insistently and asked once again where her mother was. Time was passing and Mrs. Taneran had not yet appeared, although usually she came back early from the tenant farm.

But an obstinate silence met the young woman's words. They were clearly refraining from speaking to her, and their attitude soon became so evident that she was frightened. She suddenly thought she grasped the reason for their anger and felt invaded by a sense of shame that totally crushed her. Her obsession with seeing her fears come to fruition made her recoil as if she were in the path of an object coming toward her at a dizzying speed. But just at the moment when she thought she understood, she fell back into doubt. She would have liked to have asked them a question that would have enlightened her, but nothing came to mind. They had been dwelling on their anger for too long to be able to listen to her. She realized that and decided it was more prudent to remain silent.

Nevertheless, Mrs. Pecresse could no longer contain her impatience. She leaned over Maud and hissed right in her face, "Where is your mother? She's looking for you, the poor woman! She must be very worn-out. She was already dragging herself around before that. It's because you haven't shown up the entire day, Miss Grant . . ."

Mrs. Pecresse added, cleverly calculating the effects in order to stir up shame and remorse in Maud, "In fact, she's been gone since noon hour . . ."

Maud backed away from Mrs. Pecresse, her arms stiffened in a gesture of defense, but the woman stared her down and it was the young woman who closed her eyes . . . Suddenly she saw the shadow that had crossed the cypress lane just as she was leaving George's place. Hadn't it been round and gray like the Pecresse woman herself . . . ? Was it possible that was related to what she was currently experiencing? Maud reviewed her day spent wandering near the Riotor. How had she not foreseen that during that time her brothers would remain with the Pecresses and that their desire to catch her red-handed would grow? No doubt her mother wasn't aware of anything. But they knew what they were doing. With that, there was Jacques's need to distract himself and to make her pay for the audacity she had had at Barque's the other evening.

That the Pecresse woman would collaborate with Jacques to find her guilty was unexpected, to say the least! What impudence Jacques had! He wasn't reluctant to associate with the Pecresse woman, even though he had deceived her twice, in not accepting his share of responsibility for the suicide of the young woman and in pushing his mother to leave Uderan definitively. He had clearly latched onto the first excuse to strike back at Maud, happy that she had provided him with such an ideal pretext. Up until now, he had hesitated to use sensitive arguments against her that would have also compromised himself. Since the event at Barque's, he had hung around, not finding himself at home anywhere. He felt alone and needed someone else to do something wrong in order to distract him from his own obsessive guilt . . .

Her brother knew. Maud felt lost and wanted to flee.

At that very moment, something unexpected occurred to

forcefully sweep away their anger. From the heights of Uderan came a weak, strangled voice that seemed to fear being heard, and that immediately produced silence: "Mrs. Pe-cre-sse!"

The seriousness of that call brought them together and made them feel irrelevant themselves. All of a sudden no trace of resentment was left.

"Mrs. Pe-cre-sse!" Although Mrs. Pecresse herself was the only one still taking pleasure in what she was doing, she, too, grew pale, and little by little the smile left her face. The dogs rose and perked up their ears.

When the voice grew silent, Jacques settled for shrugging his shoulders awkwardly. He didn't dare look at anyone or answer the call.

The voice came closer. "Where is my darling, my God, where is she?" After each of her cries, the voice returned to the night, like a wave returning to the sea and leaving its trace, a humid fringe.

What a failure for the Grant-Taneran brothers! They appeared stupefied that their mother would worry about their lot, even though they had let her leave without reassuring her. They became aware of their blunder, and neither of them had the strength to address this mourning expressed without indignation. "My dear Maud, my child!"

Suddenly, Henry Taneran let his jaw drop open like a deaf person who wants to hear better and said timidly, "We'd better answer her. We should have let her know . . . I myself . . ." But he didn't dare do what he was suggesting and stayed glued to his chair.

Maud didn't budge. She understood that her mother had

been calling her for hours, walking along the roads, through the fields, along the Dior.

Soon it was Maud herself who was taking to the roads, walking through tall, wet grass, following the railroad tracks . . . The heat and fatigue had finally gotten the best of Mrs. Taneran, and then, to finish it off, there was the walk along the river that evening, which buried her in the fog rising from the Dior . . . It was then that she began to call at random. Perhaps they had crossed paths without seeing each other? Without recognizing each other? With strange lucidity, Maud followed the painful path her mother had taken and could not turn aside from the sight she saw.

The voice now picked up again, first gasping for air and then filled with a tenderness that opened up like a floodgate. "My dear Maud, my child!" Maud remained petrified, having no other fear except that of feeling alive. She thought she was present at her own demise.

Soon she was back there, of course, between those white walls, with those four immovable faces, but also elsewhere, in the dark of night beside her mother. Why, though, did her mother keep on calling? Why, since she had met up with her? Maud was kissing her. She came back holding her, snuggled up against her mother's body . . .

All of a sudden, the voice was *there* in the yard.

Maud plugged her ears so she wouldn't hear it anymore, then let out a scream. In the instant that followed, all noise was suspended. The griffons began to bark. Maud fell. As she lost consciousness, she still heard the two dogs, but from afar, as if she had slowly sunken into death.

CHAPTER 12

WHEN SHE WOKE UP IN HER MOTHER'S BED, UPSTAIRS IN THE Pecresses' big, beautiful bedroom, it was almost dark. On the night table, a little lamp hidden by a newspaper offered a faint light. Maud noticed that they had put her to bed completely dressed, removing only her shoes.

She felt calm but forced herself not to think about anything, sensing that her nervousness would come back at the same time as a clear consciousness of the situation in which she found herself.

The sky, through the windows, stood out against the somber background of the bedroom and appeared as an intense blue. Gray clouds moved across it and sped toward the east, bordered by a horizon as bare as that of the high sea. A fairly strong wind was blowing and working on the trees of the yard, shaking their tops. No doubt a summer storm was brewing, which would soon erupt into a warm rain, but tomorrow the day would be as clear as ever.

When it was time to get up, Maud had to lean back against

the bed, her legs limp, her head empty. Her whole body was trembling, and she felt a profound weakness. When she opened the door, the voices of the Pecresses hit her in the face and she quickly stepped backward. Hesitating, she went from one window to the next, as if plunged in deep reflection, but in reality she wasn't thinking about anything in particular, not able to understand the sudden and fearful disarray that had overtaken her.

Soon the night had set in completely. No other noise except that of the wind came to her. The moon rose little by little in the sky, a stranger to the agitation of the earth and to the violence of the storm in the valley.

Maud suddenly felt incapable of overcoming her distress. She let herself go as if she were a drowned person floating along a river. The sound of an ongoing conversation came to her through the partially open door; she could pick up only some isolated words. No illusion was now possible: Mrs. Taneran had been advised of her daughter's flight from home.

In any case, as soon as she had been reassured concerning Maud's state, her mother must have given herself over to one of her rages that separated her from everyone else. Maud went back and looked at the lamp, whose overly bright light was subdued by the newspaper. "They didn't dare tell her right away," she thought. A feeling of great solitude heightened her emotional pain.

All at once she heard someone in clogs walking along the outer wall. The steps resonated on the hardened soil and the noise reassured her a bit, because it alone indicated that life continued with its calming, everyday activities. The heavy barn door squeaked on its hinges and shut with a huge ruckus that shook the whole house. "It must be nine o'clock," she muttered. "Mr. Pecresse is closing up his barn."

She understood all at once that she could no longer put off going downstairs, or they would lock the entrance door and she would be a prisoner until the next day. This idea brought new anxiety. "They're not going to let me out of here, not tonight, not tomorrow, not ever . . ."

Her suffering was relegated to second place in relation to this instinctive fear of being imprisoned here with them. She began to moan, with her mouth closed tightly; a groan she could not keep inside escaped from her lips, so softly that one might have thought she was humming. However, she did not stop making rapid calculations: the entranceway was unthinkable. And as for the door off the hallway, she knew it was practically sealed off. The window? It, too, was extremely high. She leaned out and quickly stepped back.

The horror she felt at finding herself once again with her family left her mind entirely clear. "There's no other way but to go downstairs," she calmly decided. Certainly, she could no longer face them with her head held high the way she used to do. But she wanted to flee from them, above all, to avoid the repulsive intimacy to which she would still be summoned, no doubt, once their anger had passed.

Her mind made up, she leaned on the windowsill a moment. The image of her lover came back to her at that point, distinct and frozen. She had no desire to see him again, sensing how useless it would be; the aversion she felt for people touched even him. His complete ignorance of what she was going through right now diminished him in her eyes, without her making the slightest effort to fight off this unjust thought.

The memory of the pleasure she had had in making love did not come back clearly, because only her memory strove to recall it, against her will. What an illusion she had had!

She imagined Durieux learning about this; she pictured the expression of worry on his face. Even if he was sincere the first few days, he would soon tire of defending her, and boredom would eat up his love to the point of leaving only the appearances. Automatically she closed the window, and at the same time the picture of her lover disappeared, after her vain effort to bring back his memory.

She groped her way downstairs and stopped behind the kitchen door. In order to find the courage to open it, she repeated to herself, "None of this is important . . . in a little while no one will be talking about it . . ."

Then she was into the room. The immediate silence swept down on her and left her disconcerted. The light was so bright that she instinctively shaded her eyes with her hand.

As everyone was sitting somewhat back from the table, they must have finished dinner. Without looking at him, she picked out Jacques, who was rolling pieces of bread between his fingers and throwing them into the fire. Near him, Mrs. Taneran probably wore the "ashen face" that her children well knew. The Pecresse woman was the first to speak. "You're going to eat something, Miss Grant . . ." The little servant girl went to get a plate, which she put on the edge of the table, and then she put some wood in the stove.

Maud wended her way toward the fireplace and leaned on it, facing the hearth, so she would no longer have to look at them. Everyone was observing a silence that became intolerable the longer it lasted, and that rose and rose, like water rising in a sinking boat. A single word would have been enough to ignite their fury, causing this deadly inertia to explode. Maud would have liked to disappear in the puddle of her shadow, dwindling until she became, like the shadow itself, nothing.

Mindlessly she tried to pet the griffon closest to her, but the dog growled, and her nervousness became such that she blushed and lost her bearings, as if this failure with the dog discredited her even more in their eyes. "Come, it's ready," said Mrs. Pecresse, "Come along, Miss Grant . . ."

Maud remained motionless, contemplating the white oval table, which sparkled in the brightness of the ceiling light, then the empty chair, and on the table, the steaming plate. Nearby, two closed, trembling hands tapped on the table: two hands with the same bone structure, palm width, and, more than anything, the distinctively inverted thumb, a sign of violence, that she bore as well. The faces in the room, plunged in the shadow of the lampshade, escaped her. The Pecresse woman pushed her toward the table, and she found herself in front of the plate.

They devoured her pitilessly with their gaze, with the curiosity inspired by every scandalous act. They followed her gestures, awaited her mistakes. The simple movement she had to make in order to eat required such an effort that, at times, she was no longer in control of her arm, which literally became paralyzed.

She would have given her life to hear them speak, at last, and say a single word that would have revealed the meaning of their anger. She knew so well the dark roads they enjoyed taking, where they got lost . . .

In the barn, which was near the kitchen, they could hear the animals crushing their bedding and rummaging around their empty feeding troughs. This familiar sound surprised Maud a little, in that it was peaceful and habitual.

Suddenly, John Pecresse got up and left. His mother, with feigned discretion, imitated him and acted as if she were following him without actually making up her mind. "You can stay, Mrs. Pecresse, you know . . ." It was the voice of Mrs. Taneran. It had a somewhat contemptuous sound to it, and more than weariness came through; it revealed such a deep discouragement that everything sank into it and disappeared like a wisp of straw.

Maud, for her part, could only fixate on her plate rather stupidly.

"What the hell do you think you're doing? Do you think we have nothing else to do but watch and wait for you?" This voice, with its skillful inflections, was that of Jacques. Maud didn't bat an eyelid.

The servant had gone to bed and Mrs. Pecresse made a move to get up and clear the table, thus feigning a noble disinterest in the whole affair. The Tanerans' disagreement was blowing up so violently that this miserable woman was very pleased and could move away from it without any effort, now that she had caused it.

"Please stay seated, Mrs. Pecresse. Maud, could you clear the table?" A feeling of hope filled the young woman, who recognized this tone of tender scolding her mother sometimes used with her.

Without a word, Maud went toward the sink. Jacques followed her closely; she heard his breathing, right there, at her back. What excuse would he come up with? The lowest, the most banal, the most ridiculous, the most shameful . . .

"So you're going to wash your plate? I'll teach you to sneak off. You don't care about anything and you've figured out how to run around . . . I won't allow it much longer . . ."

Maud kept herself from speaking or moving. The plate she held in her two hands suddenly changed its appearance, so that she no longer saw it as it was, but broken and bloody with a face coming through it, like the face of a clown bursting through a sheet of paper.

"Jacques, leave her alone; that's what she deserves," Henry chimed in.

But Jacques was in full form and impossible to stop. "We've left her alone too long! When I think of how we all indulged her, of how we trusted her . . . Do you want to know something, something I hid from you, because I had pity on her?" He stretched out his arms toward his mother in a solemn gesture. "It disgusts me that it's come to this, I must say. Do you remember? The money, when Muriel died?"

He interrupted himself, finally delivered from this very minimal obligation toward his sister. Mrs. Taneran seemed petrified. In a quick calculation, Maud measured the distance that separated her from the door. She would slip along the wall, lift the latch . . . Before rushing over, though, she summoned whatever reason she had left.

"Don't believe him; I borrowed three hundred and fifty francs in exchange for my chain bracelet—you see, I don't have it anymore . . ." She showed her bare arm and cunningly slid toward the door.

Jacques yelled like someone possessed, "It's not true, liar!"

But Maud was already outside. She hurtled down the road at such speed that the stones flew out from under her feet. When she got to the valley, near the Dior, she stopped. Insults were still being hurled at her from above. The open door shed a big square of light on the countryside. Several voices mixed together with Jacques's—that of the Pecresse woman, who yelled her name with the loud, drawling accent she had when she called her dogs in the evening. And then Henry's.

"Hey! Maud! Come back! Come stay here! If you don't, Mother won't sleep a wink. You know that, don't you . . ." Stiff, biting her lips to keep from answering, she silently shook her head—no. The first tears finally flowed from her eyes. She was soon able to see that the square of light disappeared from above.

She lay down on the riverbank. One of her hands held her head and the other hung down in the water current, making a frail and bubbly melody.

CHAPTER 13

THE WATER WAS SO COLD THAT AFTER A MOMENT MAUD could no longer feel her fingers. She withdrew her hand and put it on the thick grass, which felt warm by comparison. In the silence that reigned near the river, she heard the sound of her own sobbing. An instant later she wanted to draw up her legs, but it hurt too much; she felt the same thing when she tried to get up. Very carefully she brought her limbs in close, into the hollow of her curled-up body, discovering a gentleness in her actions that made her feel as if she had compassion for herself.

Although it was June, it was still very difficult for Maud to warm herself in this flowing rift of the Dior, where the earth softened at night like a humid sponge. Her dress and clothing stuck to her body, but it was only when she was no longer immobile that the cold penetrated her all of a sudden and made her shiver. She wasn't sad, but weary, with a weariness made painful by the cold.

Soon, the first drops of rain from the storm began to fall. She had to go in. She thought, with a stupid obstinacy, of the bed in which she had found herself after she had fainted. Was her bedroom at Uderan open? Could she go to George Durieux's place? No, anything except a return like that, which he would misinterpret.

Go to the tenant farm? Wake up the tenant farmer's daughter by knocking on the shutters? But the domestic help would get up to welcome her in, and inventing an excuse seemed beyond her capabilities.

Thus she concluded there was no other shelter but the night, right up until the morning. She didn't for a minute think about returning to the Pecresses'. This now seemed so impossible that it didn't even cross her mind.

The Dior was running beside her, young and virile, against its faithful banks. All she had to do was roll over. She would have been caught up and carried away in a moment. But that was not in her thoughts, and she would have been astonished if someone had spoken to her about suicide, because she didn't associate her despair with any thoughts of heroism. With difficulty she rose and climbed up the small hillock of the railway tracks. The rain was falling and blinding her. She took huge steps forward, stumbling and bracing herself against the moist clumps of earth; she crossed the tracks and then the road. A bright light caught her for an instant in its beam and went by quickly, as an engine roared. She didn't straighten up but continued to drag herself toward Uderan. Just as she was headed up the sloped path of the yard, she thought she sensed the presence of someone around the house. She continued, unconcerned, and stopped in front of the closed door. "I knew it—they locked it this afternoon to keep me from going back in."

She tried in vain to turn the handle. Leaning against the

door panel, she began to hit it with all her might. After every blow she waited, knowing, however, that no one would answer and how foolish her continued effort was.

All at once, a name came out of nowhere—a voice taking care not to frighten her. She stopped to answer, her voice barely registering surprise. A vague worry swept over her attentive, frozen face.

"Maud. What are you doing here? Are you crazy? I've been waiting for you all day. You left like a thief this morning." George Durieux. He was laughing, happy to have found her again, but she looked at him gravely, not understanding why he was there.

"Oh, thank goodness it's you. I wasn't expecting you, you know."

In the glow of his flashlight, he saw that she was pale, with a gaze that revealed an extreme fatigue. His laugh was suddenly cut short.

She took refuge against the door, as if expressing with her body what she didn't have the strength to say. He was embarrassed by her odd behavior. "What do you want? Say something!"

"George, I would like you to open this door. I promise that tomorrow I will explain everything to you, but for the moment, open this door. They've closed it, and I'm tired."

He rattled the door without succeeding in opening it. "You can see it's not going to open," he said, shaking his head. "Listen, listen to me, will you . . ." She left after making a sign for him to wait.

He heard her go down the path that led to the abandoned greenhouse in the main part of the building and ferret around in the big mass of scrap metal and wood below the shed. He stayed where he was, unable to resist her request.

It was late. What was she doing still outside? Wasn't it clear? She'd been running around with someone. John, perhaps . . .? He suddenly wanted to leave. When he recalled how naturally she had offered herself to him the night before, he was overwhelmed by disillusionment.

She appeared, moreover, not very concerned about him. As she hadn't come back up, he imagined she must be groping around in the dark. Suddenly remembering the logs that the tenant famer had piled above the scrap metal, he worried that the pile might have fallen on her. He imagined her struggling under the wood and ran toward the stairs. Then, by the feeble light of his flashlight, he saw her come back up, with a bar of iron in her hand. "Here, do it with this!"

George shoved the bar into the crack that separated the two door panels, and it opened with a loud bang that echoed into the empty rooms. When he saw her in the bright light, he noticed the upheaval in her features and the change that had brusquely occurred in their expression. Maud's gray eyes had almost disappeared under her swollen eyelids, and the very appearance of her face seemed ruined. Her mouth, pale and chapped, wet strands of hair strewn all over, and the big dirty stain that soiled her damp dress all made her unrecognizable.

His feelings for her were no match for this challenge. He didn't even try to understand. He stood in front of her without moving.

She lay down, pulling the sheet up under her chin in a childlike, egotistical movement that shoved him firmly out of her thoughts. She asked him something, her eyes half-closed.

He drew the heavy curtains, then lit a little oil lamp on the night table, filling the room with a flickering glow.

At last he sat down near the pedestal table and, as Maud had done the night before, examined the room, looking mechanically at this sad, luxurious decor. Usually she received him in the dining room. Everywhere a thick layer of dust was visible, from the canopy on the four-poster bed to the garnet-colored curtains.

She didn't say anything more. Her breathing was so regular that he thought she was asleep, and suddenly this sleep represented all of human perversion for him. She was hiding from his questions. "Maud, are you ever going to say something to me?"

She stretched painfully but smiled, refreshed by this first plunge into sleep. "I'm sure it's the Pecresse woman; I saw her this morning at the end of the lane when I was leaving your place . . ." He jumped up and pushed her to answer his questions in a voice that was curt and crisp.

"At what time did you leave . . . ? How did they make you understand that . . . ?"

He didn't wait for the answer, finally deducing, through his questions, what she had hidden from him. Then, with a gentler voice, he queried, "You ran away from them, didn't you?" Without speaking, she hid her face in her pillow.

Standing at the foot of her bed, he watched her sleep. His long silhouette leaned over to see her better. She seemed to be watching him ironically, through her thick eyelashes, the shadow of which the light of the little lamp lengthened right down to her cheeks. He would never have thought that a sleeping face could have such a moving profile. The thought that she had slept a whole night at his side troubled him as much as if he hadn't known her.

She had been courting danger for weeks now, but what had *he* done to deserve her silence? He naturally shied away from her.

Occasionally the room was refreshed by a waft of air from the poorly shut door. Maud turned over and over again in bed. From time to time she smiled or murmured some indistinct words.

For the first time, George thought wearily about the next day. He calculated precisely the violence of the crossfire that The Pardal and the Pecresse woman were aiming at Maud and would have liked to escape it.

A deep peace still reigned over the countryside and the grounds. George left, suddenly worried that with the arrival of dawn someone might find him there. The frosty air gave off an earthy smell. He breathed it in with all his might. A feeling of freedom overtook him. Wasn't he being a little ridiculous? He was going to have some problems with the family, but it was in Jacques's best interest to spare him . . . the unfolding of events would help him; the Tanerans would not take long to leave. Uderan would be sold. Maud would disappear.

Yet for an instant, he wished that she would reappear one more time before their departure.

CHAPTER 14

IT WAS A BEAUTIFUL DAY. MAUD HAD SPRUCED HERSELF UP, washed the stain off her dress, and arranged her hair. As soon as she was outside the house, the heat soaked into her body and did her good.

On the road to the tenant farmer's home, the trees projected rounded and already shortened shadows, indicating it was close to noon. On each side of the road, a series of small hills stretched out, of which the pathway lined with fruit trees in the middle of the Uderan plateau constituted the central backbone.

The old Uderan house was partially hidden from Maud by the curve in the road. Too big, almost unusable, it featured sprawling bare walls on which, at regular intervals, high windows with blinds were lined up. On account of these walls, no longer in alignment, and the bumpy roof, one might have said that it had succumbed to the pressure of an inner force that it once resisted. Fundamentally, though, it was still quite solid. It had been built by wealthy farmers from The Pardal and represented the patience and frugality of farm folk. People in The Pardal said that five brothers and sisters had contributed to the cost of its construction at the end of the seventeenth century. Much later, the property had been bought by a bourgeois landowner who had planted the grounds around it.

Now the local farmers laughed at it because Uderan had never fallen into good hands. What they were envious of was the land around it, because little by little, through the centuries, they had become indifferent to all forms of riches but those that yield a profit. "I ask you, who would want to live in it! It would hold ten families, not to speak of the land. But you would have to look pretty far to find a buyer for the house . . ." Only the Pecresse woman wanted to move her son there, not finding anything worthy of this genius in the towns of Semoic and The Pardal.

The tenant farmer's wife spotted Maud and promptly came toward her. Mrs. Dedde was dark-haired and still young, with a glowing, fine-featured face revealing minuscule veins crisscrossing her cheeks. She had aged considerably and lost weight in the last ten years, and the softened flesh around her arms looked like a piece of overripe fruit, while on her neck, small, silky creases now formed when she spoke.

She was rather surprised to see Maud at such an unusual hour but kept from showing her curiosity . . . "Can I offer you something, Miss Maud?"

"That would be lovely, Mrs. Dedde, whatever you have." Maud blushed in spite of herself.

The woman served her and was happy to see her drink down a cup of café au lait with such satisfaction. While attending to her work, she kept glancing over at Maud. She had known

Maud as a child and liked her well enough, although the girl probably wasn't too much to her fancy. She preferred Henry to her, because the tenant farmer's wife had been there when he was born and had nursed him at the same time as her daughter.

"What's that sound?" asked Maud. "Is that the animals?"

"Yes," Mrs. Dedde replied, "my daughter is at mass, and the animals are anxious to get outside in this beautiful weather." Then, in the most natural way, she went on, "By the way, I think your mother was looking for you yesterday; she seemed very worried, the poor woman; she had no reason to, as I told her. How nervous she is these days!"

"It's because my brother changed his mind," Maud said brusquely. "He no longer intends to stay here. Hadn't you heard? You can understand that it bothers Mother, after all the expenses we have incurred recently . . . As for me, I think we should sell now."

"I don't like to say it, miss, but your mother lacks authority. Don't you think she should have realized it was time to sell? And those pieces of furniture waiting at Semoic? It hurts us, too, to hear what people are saying . . . Mrs. Pecresse came to tell Dedde that she herself had paid for them and doesn't want anyone going after them. If she had only said it to us . . . But that Pecresse woman is doing everything she can to harm you. It surprises me that she does that, because she's intelligent and it's not in her interest to let you go."

Maud didn't leave, even though she had finished eating. The farmer's wife noticed her staring at the Pecresse place. The young woman thought it useless to explain why she wasn't at mass, that she was afraid of running into her family there.

Mrs. Dedde went out for a moment and came back with a big bucket, the contents of which she poured into a pot. "Look! My girl's coming back already from the first mass!" She seemed to be reflecting and struck the joyful tone of someone who has found the exact words she wants to express. "I forgot to tell you, Miss Maud, that your friend Louise Rivière is on holidays here. Maybe you could go and see her."

As Maud headed slowly toward the door, Mrs. Dedde muttered, "You know, when it comes to eating, whenever you like, miss . . ." Maud turned around and forced herself to smile. The farmer's wife had guessed something, and the young woman was troubled.

She decided to go and see Louise Rivière. Since her arrival, Maud had not really visited with anyone, and for lack of anything better to do, this visit would take up her afternoon. Mrs. Dedde was right.

Maud arrived at the edge of the descent formed by the Uderan fields above the Riotor. Instinctively she began to run, but finding it useless to run like that, she slowed down to a walk. The little home of Mrs. Rivière, hanging solidly onto the other side of the valley, did not attract her very much.

Louise was the daughter of a war veteran's widow, who, by dint of sacrifice, had brought her up very respectably. In fact, she was the only child of the village to have spent time with Maud Grant. And, although Louise had come to Uderan every Thursday, it was possible that it hadn't interested her that much.

Maud retained a fading memory of this pallid child in her schoolgirl pinafore. Louise missed the fields and the surrounding meadows where she would have liked to play and mingle with the other village children. By means of trickery, Maud would try to detain this girl who frequented the school and amassed in her little pug-nosed head endless pieces of schoolgirl gossip. Maud, for her part, had not yet gone to school and only studied haphazardly with her mother. When she was with the young Uderan girl, Louise remained locked up and silent, her arms crossed behind her back, waiting to be amused. She barely consented, toward the end of the afternoon, to rock a doll, but nervously, as if she were just clowning about. When it came time to return home, she took off excitedly. Maud accompanied her friend to the Riotor and then climbed back up the hill, sauntering around until nightfall.

She didn't feel any curiosity now at seeing Louise again, only some embarrassment . . . The two women were finishing lunch. Mrs. Rivière was busy in the dining room and Louise was humming in a rocking chair. Perfect order and simplistic taste revealed the presence of two women alone in the house. Mrs. Rivière stopped short and said with a lack of surprise in her voice, "Well! Here's Maud."

She offered Maud two pale and slightly greasy cheeks above the pile of dishes she was carrying. Louise gave a cry of surprise and jumped up noisily, assuming an exaggerated look of contentment. Despite the makeup, which no doubt enhanced Louise's looks, Maud would have had no trouble anywhere recognizing this small face with its unhealthy complexion, cold eyes, and tight mouth that twisted when she spoke.

"Mrs. Dedde told me that you had come home from Bordeaux, so I came over," said Maud. Without being invited, she fell into a chair and wiped her forehead with the back of her bare, cool arm.

"How nice of you," exclaimed Louise. "In fact, I had promised myself to go and see you at the Pecresses'. That's where you're staying, isn't it?"

They exchanged small talk. Between each topic of conversation that was quickly exhausted, the time passed stifling and heavy for Maud. Some stray flies flew around, periodically hitting the windows and falling lifeless below. The oppressiveness of summer bore down upon the house and its surroundings, motionless, almost white with intensity. She would have to wait until the most trying moment of the day had passed, the peak of the heat. Maud didn't have the strength to leave. And this powerlessness to flee even farther away disheartened her.

Mrs. Rivière and her daughter were amazed to see Maud so silent. They exchanged surprised glances. The mother asked Maud for news of Mrs. Taneran. Maud scrutinized their faces to gauge the sincerity of their smiles, which reminded her of the fixed reading on a barometer. She replied that her mother had never been better.

She then dutifully reminded Louise of their common memories. Did she remember their Thursdays at Uderan, those sad Thursdays? Yes, she had changed, and looked prettier, certainly. The sentences and laughs of the two women flew over Maud's head like birds you can't identify but are part of the landscape. She had a hard time registering their words and only succeeded from time to time.

Louise stood out against the window as she continued to rock in her chair. The heat and the sun that had begun to creep underneath the blind on the door rendered her cheeks bright red. She glittered with all sorts of jewelry. She was perhaps only noticeable on account of this showy paraphernalia, and maybe also her well-proportioned body, exceptionally slender and agile, with a supple waist, which seemed to invite the touch of a hand.

Beyond the permanent characteristics of her face, Maud finally detected a change in Louise. Likable for no particular reason, Louise had increased in falseness, in flirtatiousness. She overflowed with a fawning affability, already as ingrained in her as in the manners of a grown woman. One felt she had matured through powers of reflection and calculation uncommon in a young woman. At twenty-two, she was not yet married, though two years older than Maud. In the two villages, few claimants would have suited her, on the one hand in terms of her education, which outclassed them, and on the other, in terms of her finances, which were slim, even nonexistent. Still young, she already suffered atrociously from the fear of growing old. She was torn between excessive ambition and the despair of not living up to it. Her evident nervousness made this dilemma both tragic and irritating.

Louise wanted to go to The Pardal and began skillfully trying to persuade Maud to accompany her. The idea of this outing obviously did not please Mrs. Rivière. Louise led her friend outside and briefly explained: "I have to go. It's really lucky that you came. You have to agree . . ."

Maud accepted. Louise ran up to the house and when she returned threw herself flat out on the grass. The permission she had just obtained filled her with such violent satisfaction that she felt faint, as well as happy and relaxed, at the prospect of her pleasure.

The hottest hours had passed and the breeze picked up. "You understand, Maud, it's at the end of vespers. I can't miss the moment people are coming out . . . You'll never guess . . ." Maud didn't press her to continue or try to draw out any confidences. She felt calm and her mind was a blank. Stretched out with her arms folded as a pillow under her head, she listened. "You know, Maud, you're going to be surprised and likely not all that happy. It's your brother Jacques who is going to be waiting for me at the end of vespers . . ." Louise's face became serious, and a certain ferocity appeared.

"It's all the same to me, Louise; why should I care?" replied Maud.

"Imagine, he came by in the afternoon yesterday. I was watching the cow. He asked me specifically if I had seen you . . ." Louise paused. Maud didn't respond, and Louise began again, in a confidential tone of voice. "We talked, and he asked me to come at the end of vespers. We're going to take a walk together . . ." Lying flat on her stomach, Louise reveled in her feelings of delight.

Maud, who was looking up, didn't blink in the sun. Fluffy clouds were gathering in the pure blue sky, which kept changing toward the south. Just contemplating it was a cause for joy. Louise's voice, frail and piercing, didn't stop. "Oh, your brother's a pretty swell guy, you know . . . And chic! Not like the simpletons around here!"

"What are you trying to say to me?" asked Maud. "If it's about Durieux, you can go ahead . . ." Louise smiled stupidly and blushed a little. In reality, that interested her less than her own story.

"Mother doesn't believe it—she likes you a lot. I do too, in fact, but I would understand certain things very well. I'm very liberated, you know. And then people say such bizarre things about you folks, about you . . ." She didn't add anything because Maud found it pointless to encourage her.

Louise rolled over on her back and looked at the sky, her eyes blinking. They really didn't have anything to say to each other. Both recognized that their friendship no longer existed, that since their childhood, and in spite of what they may have done to encourage it, their feelings had turned into an extreme dislike.

It was a fine day in June, despite the heat. Because of the recent rains, the grass was thick and luscious, and the air gave off the fragrance of sap. Thrushes flew low over the fields and the velvety whir of their wings made a rustling noise. From the tops of the tall poplar trees of the Riotor, goldfinches were singing, infusing the azure sky with their voluptuous, triumphant notes. The cries of other birds rang out far and near, piercing or modulating, and one had to listen carefully to distinguish a single cry from so many. Surrounded by the woods of Uderan, the silence seemed to repose on these innumerable murmurs of birds. Sometimes, similar to the unfolding of a dying wave, puffs of warm air traversed the foliage of the trees.

Without warning, the bells of The Pardal rang out. Not a particle of air escaped their vibration; not a blade of grass or a leaf failed to quiver. As Maud didn't move, Louise sat up, this time authoritatively. Her mouth tightened with sudden anger, and she cried out, "Well? Vespers are sounding; don't forget what you promised. If I want to be there when people are leaving, we have to leave right away."

Maud said simply, "If I hadn't come, what would you have done? Just run! I'll take care of your mother if she asks for you." Louise hesitated and then made up her mind. But before leaving she asked a question she had kept to herself until then, for fear of losing Maud's complicity.

"Is it true that you're selling the property?" Maud made an evasive sign. "And it's because of you? You can pretend the contrary; it's Jacques who told me. I'm warning you, everyone here is on his side—we know him well. Oh, I know you're full of pride."

Standing tall, she glared at Maud, who was still lying down at her feet; never before would she have spoken with such boldness. Now she took such intense pleasure in it that she went beyond her own intention to be mean. She heard herself speak and closed her eyes rapturously after every sentence that she spewed out.

"And John Pecresse's fiancée? That poor abandoned girl? Do you think she fell into the Dior from Barque's deck, foolishly, just like that? You're lucky she has no one looking out for her, filthy lucky . . ."

Maud felt that Louise was poised at the height of her rage, as if at the summit of a balcony from which she was contemplating her victim. Louise then left abruptly, after having tried in vain to strike a final, masterful blow. "After all, I feel sorry for you! So long!"

Louise ran toward The Pardal, her arms swinging, not once looking back. Maud blinked softly and watched her leave. She again pictured Louise's small, vicious face, plastered against the sky, vomiting the insult.

CHAPTER 15

LITTLE BY LITTLE, AFTER LOUISE'S DEPARTURE, THE DAY, TOO, began to slip away. On the other side of the Riotor, smoke from the chimneys of The Pardal and the Uderan tenant farm delicately wafted up into the calm sky; after stretching out for an instant, it turned and climbed over the oak forest that overshadowed the village.

The dinner hour was approaching, and Sunday ended at the very moment when the men went in and didn't come back out. Louise still hadn't returned, even though vespers had been over for a long time.

Maud wondered what this gentleness that arose with the evening was, so hard on her heart. Without really seeing it, she looked at this landscape where her childhood had unfolded: the majestic pinewood with its stringent layout, as high as a church nave; the Riotor that sank down into the lower prairies like a blade. One could hear its rapid, muffled babbling fill the valley right up to the edge.

Maud thought about the fact that her mother and brothers

would soon be coming back from The Pardal. But she was too far away to see them go by. She heard Mrs. Rivière's door close and the shutters being folded in. The woman didn't call, but Maud guessed that she came from time to time to the threshold of the door to check the road from The Pardal. She didn't see Maud, who was waiting in the field behind the house, down below.

How had Maud's story become common knowledge? Despite what Louise had said, Maud thought it was the Pecresse woman who had been spreading it around. She felt such repugnance for this woman that her own family suddenly appeared gifted with unexpected qualities in comparison. She was sure they hadn't said anything. Jacques himself remained discreet when it came to his family. They were united by a secret solidarity that made them a real family . . .

And she herself was part of this clan, no matter what she did. She was tempted to go back, to bring an end to her stupid, wandering attempt to run away. But stubbornness fastened her to the ground. Even more important, she didn't see what she could do to find her place again in the midst of her family, or how to hold her own beside Jacques and her mother.

What would become of her? Without the daily problems she encountered living at home, she would have difficulty getting used to a peaceful existence. Their general condemnation didn't frighten her. On the contrary, she believed it to be justified. People who were indifferent and fickle now scared her more.

Her isolation had a greater impact on her than her brother's meanness, or the unflattering treatment she received from

Taneran, whose verbal attacks she could easily ward off. She would have come back to her mother, but Jacques, a formidable opponent, was probably standing guard against the new enemy, emboldened by her mistake.

Disgust kept her from returning, disgust for her brother and for the legitimate grievance he now had against her. What place did this man have in their familiar world, exercising more control every day! Since they had left Paris, he no longer inspired terror in her, because she judged him in a more detached way. It was hard to imagine how this aging child could ever leave his mother and the family that defined him, or the care and honor that surrounded him there. Elsewhere, he lacked boldness, letting himself be terrorized by other people.

It was difficult for Maud to think about Jacques without still feeling a sudden surge of horror. She couldn't remember being able to look him once in the eyes or daring to confront him alone without trembling. He failed to perceive the repulsion his sister felt for him. Once his anger passed, he always willingly returned to her. This disarming forgetfulness, this self-satisfaction that nothing could disturb, exasperated Maud even more than his insults.

Since the death of his wife, their mutual animosity had worsened to the point that, in a way, their lives were simplified. The memory of the loan Jacques had never repaid and that Maud never talked about irritated Jacques like an unpardonable fault on his part. The night before, lacking in valid arguments, he had used this pretext, unable to countenance the idea that Maud could claim to have anything at all against him.

Until then, no excuse had seemed enough to justify the explosion of a hatred that grew more violent every day. What excuses would have been powerful enough to justify a resentment that had no need of motives? Jacques's bitterness had become partially unreal or imaginary for them, and they had been ready to accept it, as one does in adopting dreadful but convenient hypotheses that leave one feeling comfortable if they are not examined too closely.

Maud was somewhat unhappy with her own futile behavior, which troubled the peace formerly existing between Jacques and herself.

Louise came back alone from The Pardal, and Maud understood by her demeanor that something upsetting had taken place. She walked toward Maud, cynical and determined. Louise's eyes were swollen, and her face, bathed now in tears, was changed into a startlingly angry mask, bearing little resemblance to her normal appearance. All radiance had disappeared, suggesting that the glow that usually transfigured her was due only to the feverish expectation of pleasure.

"He didn't even look at me!" Louise cried out. "He only had eyes for that big, silly goose, the Dedde girl, who was with him and your mother . . ." Louise's pronouncement tore Maud from her daydream, obliging her to look at Louise and opine on what had just happened.

"Sit down a moment," Maud finally said. "You can't go in looking like that. You were saying that he was with the Dedde girl?"

Louise confirmed her account, shamelessly exhibiting her disappointment. It wasn't her first letdown. The young people mocked her, and she sought in vain ways to get back at them. "Still, nobody has done that to me. He turned his eyes toward me, yet he didn't even seem to see me. I didn't dare approach him, because of your mother." Maud guessed that Mrs. Dedde, the tenant farmer's wife, had sent her daughter to inform Jacques and Mrs. Taneran of Maud's visit. As to Jacques's uncouthness, it had long ceased to amaze her.

"Don't cry," Maud said. "He'll soon be tired of the Dedde girl and won't be long in coming back to you. In two or three days at the most, if that's what you want." But Louise stood up. "You make me sick!" she screamed. "Maybe *you* would accept that! Of course you would, because you run around with Durieux, who's had all the girls in the region after him. Oh, you people have no dignity, you're just trash . . ."

On that note, Louise left. Any other words would have surprised Maud, but the sincerity, violence, and spontaneity of this way of talking satisfied her.

After Louise's departure, solitude once again filled the narrow prairie invaded by shadows. In reality night was slow in coming, but for Maud its onslaught was brutal and decisive. She felt she was suddenly waking up in the dark. Lights shone in the distance on the horizon. The birds had stopped their chorus, but from the surrounding thickets came the chirping of crickets and mysterious sounds of flight. She heard a train whistle in the distance: the last train from Bordeaux, the one that left at nine o'clock. In her childhood, it was usually from a warm kitchen or during a peaceful evening that she heard the call of the engine. It whistled several times at regular intervals, separated by veritable gulfs of silence, at the bottom of which obscure dangers and muffled threats seemed to lurk. The train cars descended the slope of the plateau toward Semoic with the infernal screeching of metal. The curve was dangerous, as it was always enveloped in fog and hidden by the alders of Uderan. One could imagine the sudden appearance of this locomotive monster born of the mist and the woods.

Durieux's house was reasonably far from where Maud found herself. To reach it she was obliged to descend and then go back up the pastures of the Riotor. She then took the sunken road along the flat part, cut across the fields of alfalfa, and crossed the village.

CHAPTER 16

ARRIVING IN FRONT OF GEORGE DURIEUX'S HOUSE, MAUD stopped short, as abruptly as a machine. At the end of the lane of cypress trees, hiding the front door, a car was waiting. Friends, no doubt, having come from Bordeaux on this beautiful Sunday.

Maud hesitated. No valid pretext to justify her visit to George's came to mind. Moreover, what excuses could shelter her from the perceptiveness of the visitors, who would guess, she believed, if only from her appearance, her pitiful affair. Her misery seemed to cling to her body like a stubborn smell. Her wrinkled dress, her dirty shoes, proclaimed her situation as well as her face, which she felt was tired and drawn.

Yet she couldn't make up her mind to leave. Where would she go? She fearfully imagined the coming night, which she would spend trudging through the countryside. The thought of her stuffy bedroom at Uderan made her shudder with disgust. Hunger and fatigue were already tormenting her mind and body. Didn't she overcome fear, just a short while ago, in climbing back up from the Riotor? After being alone, her own presence tortured her, and she wanted to be with George again.

Making her way halfway up the lane, she waited. George didn't come out, and time went by without Maud admitting her impatience to herself. A moment passed and the moon appeared. Maud left the middle of the lane and went to lean against the side of the house. After the darkness of the twilight, the gentle light that suddenly illuminated the landscape comforted her.

On the side of the house opposite the one she was on, light shone out the open windows. Inside, people were talking and laughing, but she had trouble picking out George's voice, which rarely mixed with the conversation. Her weariness was so great that whenever laughter broke out, she felt its impact viscerally in her body, painfully.

No specific thought engaged her mind, but rather, numerous contrary impressions arose, one after the other, disconnected and out of control on account of her weak, confused state. But as all these feelings flowed through her, they left her each time with a greater sense of calm and understanding.

Thus, even though she didn't consider turning back, her brother's attitude took on a different meaning in the new order of things she had just discovered. Circumstances alone had defined the man he was, hard and abnormal, capable of all kinds of base acts. She finally grasped the weakness of his defenses against her, against an imaginary danger that possessed him.

Suddenly dogs barked joyfully in the distance and she recognized the twin voices of the Pecresses' griffons. The pale

light of a storm lantern appeared at the top of the path join-
ing Uderan to the Pecresse property. If they were looking for
her, she had ample time to flee. The idea that someone was
worried about her touched her a little. Tears filled her eyes
and traced fresh furrows on her cheeks. They weren't happy
either, over there. No one had ever been happy in her family.
They lived in disorder, and their passions gave the simplest
events a tragic, singular twist, which increasingly took away
the hope of ever possessing happiness.

After making one another suffer, they sought one another
out and brought each one back, by will or by force. This final
remorse alone demonstrated that they held each other in a
certain regard, and that one's absence would leave a void in
the home. These thoughts touched her at first, but it didn't
take long for her to resist her emotions.

No, she wouldn't go back. It was totally useless now that she
understood how their attachment manifested itself. Jacques
took pleasure in humiliating his victims; then he did his best
to reassure them, so that he would not completely lose them.
No, she would never, ever go back.

But hadn't they called her? The specter of her mother passed
through her mind, so tender in her memory, warm like the
thought of summer's return when one is still in winter. Maud
didn't move, but she couldn't prevent a few tears from falling.

Soon, moreover, the light of the lamp disappeared from
the Uderan grounds. A fairly long time passed before it reappeared on the plateau. Those searching for her were probably
coming back below the road, along the Dior.

"We'll see if she's at Uderan or somewhere on the road,"
Mrs. Taneran must have said. "If she's elsewhere, too bad . . . "

They wouldn't look for her at George Durieux's, she knew that much.

Her courage returned all of a sudden. She knocked on the door. As no one answered, she pushed it open and stood without moving on the doorstep, immediately seized by the desire to flee.

In the light that blinded her, she could not pick out anyone at first. After a few seconds, someone noticed her and gave a little cry of surprise. At that point, George came up to her. In his mind, he quickly calculated the immensity of the distress that must have brought her back to him. He had always hoped she would come back, but embarrassed for the moment, he set those reasons aside. As she didn't say anything, he feared she would escape before he could reach her.

"Come and sit down, come," he said quietly. The authority of his voice was concealed by the familiarity of his tone.

Once Maud was in the light, he realized that she was beautiful and that people would find her so, despite her strange attitude. He had often picked up wounded animals when he was hunting in the woods. Their expression was identical to Maud's: a lost, surprised look, with mysterious intensity. It was as if they wanted to communicate an infinitely valuable discovery as they were losing consciousness, and understood the life they could have lived had they been aware of the evil that threatened them and had just killed them.

George felt proud of Maud's beauty. Even though, in his cruel and thoughtless ways as a man, he might have killed her too, he felt joy to have conquered her again, and he introduced her with confidence. "Miss Grant, you know, from the Uderan estate."

Maud did her best to try to please him. She stayed quiet and wore a smile on her face like a mask, without it touching her eyes. Now that she found herself at George's, at the end of her mad dash to get away, she felt good. The guests didn't interest her; she barely saw them, in fact, but waited patiently for their departure . . .

CHAPTER 17

THE AFTERNOON WAS THE BEST PART OF THE DAY.

In front of her, the landscape rose in a broad, slow movement right up to the crest of Uderan, and the house looked as if it were staggering under the assault of this wave of land. As she was getting up, Maud caught sight of Uderan in the foreground of this landscape, and beyond it, the Dior valley and the Pecresse home, of which only the roof appeared. The Pardal was below the wave, so to speak, and not visible to her.

She held in her hands a book she wasn't reading. If perchance someone passed by the gap at the end of the lane of cypress trees, she automatically withdrew from the window, emotionless, and hid behind the wall for a moment; then she took her regular place again . . .

When George had left, at the beginning of the afternoon, there was no one left but the old servant, who made monotonous noises in the kitchen, downstairs on the main floor. Sometimes she spoke to herself, and it was reassuring to hear her, even if Maud knew the woman was complaining about her. But the woman soon left too, closing the door with the turn of a key, and Maud very clearly heard the muffled sound of her footsteps moving alongside the wall . . .

The heat stagnated around the house, like a pond. In the beginning, Maud had tried to stay in the main room downstairs, but she quickly gave up and went back upstairs. She desperately needed to see this landscape, which, though partly obscured, reached a distant horizon, and beyond the Dior River, a land flat and full of light, abounding in poplars. On certain days, the heat was such that it literally rose like smoke from the wheat fields and glowed in a huge, vertical expanse of shimmering color through which the landscape seemed to weep.

From time to time, Maud was seized with fleeting anxiety. Someone was knocking on the door downstairs or else the dogs were barking. She woke up from her torpor. The feeling of approaching danger had become a kind of unnerving distraction for her in this undisturbed calm. When she succeeded in reading a little or in concentrating briefly on one thing or another, she found herself afterward in a state of profound stupefaction. The reasons for her flight seemed childish to her. She hadn't been duped, but she liked to imagine that she had been. A hope took hold in her, and she would easily have laughed or cried out if she hadn't been so alone. Generally she didn't read for very long, having a hard time following the thread of the story; the effort quickly discouraged her, despite her typically determined will.

For more than two weeks, no one had come to ask about her. When George went to town, the farmers didn't show any curiosity toward him. A knowing silence surrounded them.

He had learned from them, however, that Uderan had been put up for sale and that several buyers were interested. But they were careful not to say anything about Maud.

He left her alone during the day and came back from Semoic only at dinnertime, staggering from tiredness and sometimes a little drunk. The dinner took place without him speaking a word to her, acting indifferent to her presence, and barely looking at her when she spoke to him.

One evening when he returned, George found Maud in the room downstairs. Crouched on the sofa, she was looking for a book on the shelf and was embarrassed to be found there by him; she normally didn't come down until he called for her at mealtime.

They had been unhappy since her return and avoided each other. Maud found as much instability in George's life as in her own. In the beginning, she hadn't tried to discover the secret behind his behavior toward her. In fact, she couldn't imagine any other way of doing things: if he showed pleasure from having her with him, he would lose her. Thus, he observed total discretion, and even if he suffered, that only proved that the experience wasn't completely in vain and bore at least some bitter fruit.

But that evening, Maud would have liked to speak freely to George, without holding back. The time had come for them to talk, and to put an end, one way or another, to the uncertainty of their lives. Boredom and solitude did not blind her, even though they made her suffer, and she knew that only time would bring a conclusion to their adventure.

But she was disconcerted by George, because he didn't seem to expect anything from the days that went by. He didn't talk about staying or leaving and fell more and more into silence. Even during the night, when he came to her, he stayed the same—harsh and inconsistent; as a result, she, too, came to share in his extravagant behavior, with a pleasure that always astonished her flesh and whose dark memories seemed barely perceptible when daylight came.

When he surprised her in the downstairs room that evening, she saw that he was tired and perhaps happy to find her. He brushed his hand across her face, slowly threw his hat on the couch, and then asked her, "What time is it? Do you know? These evenings never seem to end . . ." He collapsed on a chair near the table, obviously not expecting a response to his question.

"You came in earlier than usual," replied Maud. "You see, Amelia hasn't set the table yet. I came looking for a book on your bookshelf because . . ." She despaired again as she saw him distance himself from her, as little concerned with her presence as if he lived in a dream in which she had no part. However, he loved her. The proof of this was the desperate determination he put into having her each night, without taking the easy pleasure men usually so willingly allow themselves. But whatever she did, nothing counted in his eyes except that certainty that she did not feel strong enough to give him.

Nevertheless, she felt it was up to her to approach him, because he would never make any effort to understand her. Things weighed on him without his trying to react to them. Thus, at Barque's, she had already noticed, shouldn't he have gotten rid of John Pecresse for her? By the same token, during a very long month, he had fled her because Jacques had announced to him the engagement of his sister to John. Shouldn't he have disregarded that and come to see her? Even if he was like Jacques in some ways, he didn't have Jacques's stubbornness, and Maud didn't know quite what to think of him.

"Because?" he asked her, partially standing. "Because you want to read? Why would you want to? You must have a reason . . ."

"Because I'm bored," she countered. "Oh, I'm terribly bored, you know! You leave me alone . . ."

He reflected, and replied in a soft voice, "If I didn't leave you, our situation would be even worse. All you can do is be patient." She didn't fully understand the meaning of his words but guessed he was trying to speak kindly.

"So, what do you like to read? If you like, I can bring you some books from Semoic." She grabbed the cover of the old hardback book and read aloud, "*The Valley of the Moon*. It's by Jack London."

"You haven't read that?" he said. "You should read, Maud; you have nothing else to do here . . ."

"I don't have much fun reading. Or else I have sudden urges to do it . . . ," she confessed.

George shook his head like someone digesting upsetting news. "I saw your brother Jacques at Semoic. He's incredibly bored. I think that's why he was so solicitous. He doesn't care about scandal and has no self-esteem. He's a despicable person. It makes me sick to let you go; you can't imagine what it's like . . . all the more so because he's probably angry at you. You should have gone back to Paris a lot sooner; you're the one holding them back . . ."

Once again, without seeming to do so, he was asking her the question in theory. She stopped him with a small, dramatic gesture. "I'm sure that if they aren't leaving, it's in order to sell Uderan. They wouldn't put themselves out for me. Don't give me that . . ."

He got up. She hadn't responded, not yet. It was likely she wouldn't stay. He made a weary motion and added with a calm and resolute voice, "I'm going down to the river, Maud, while I wait for dinner."

She tried to hold him back and ran after him. "Just a minute, George, just a minute." He looked at her for a moment, in the muted and sulfurous light of the setting sun: her summer dress, faded and too short, revealed her smooth bare legs in her black city shoes; her long, lifeless hair hung in disorder. Her eyes were truly an indescribable gray, which in the bright light showed off her slightly mauve pallor; that precious skin, more than living, was delicately active, only letting the most discreet nuances of her blood filter through the blues and the mauves . . . For the first time, he saw in her a deceitful look, in a pleading face with a forced smile.

"If you'd like, George, I could go with you. It's going to be night soon; no one will see us . . ." He came back to her, caressed her hand and kissed it. "I haven't gone out for two weeks," she pleaded. "You don't seem to understand. We could walk together until dinner, as we did in the past . . ."

He shook his head, remaining intransigent, and was a bit surprised that she insisted so much. He suddenly saw in her such beauty that it was, in itself, enough of a promise. This beauty was still unknown to her, moreover, and to most of the people who knew her, but the greatest of beauties needs to know herself in order to assert herself.

He refused to let her accompany him. "In a little while you won't remember anything, whereas for me . . . You suspect as much, don't you? Please forgive me for the nights . . . When I come home from Semoic, I have to admit, it's impossible for me not to go up and find you—as long as you're here, between these four walls . . ."

She lowered her eyes and didn't insist anymore. In moving away from her, he thought that, even if she was still innocent in many respects, she was neither sugary nor sentimental like most girls her age. He was amazed at her slightly disdainful candor and her refusal to lie to him.

When he reached the road, at the end of the cypress tree lane, he turned around. She was still there. He remembered he had something serious to tell her and came back.

"I don't know why I would hide from you a matter that concerns you. Uderan has been bought by the Pecresses . . . bought, in a manner of speaking. They're crazy. They're rich, of course, but all the same! . . . They must have put everything they had and even what they didn't have into it. The conditions of the sale are outrageous . . ."

"I've been ready for anything, and I admit that I suspected something," responded Maud.

"They say your mother is quite short on money; she'll still be keeping the house in her name, as well as all the land except the vineyards, which she handed over. The Pecresses agreed to take over running everything and to pay her a usage fee, which the Deddes never paid. They also consented to an advance of almost fifty thousand francs on the purchase of the vineyards."

Maud thought of the Deddes. What would become of them? "The Deddes left last week," continued George. "I saw the daughter the night before last, at Barque's; your mother gave them something to compensate them."

When she was alone again, Maud mechanically picked up the book she had chosen. As she was going upstairs, the servant was entering the dining room to set the table.

Why did George find his revelations crazy? Certainly, the terms seemed advantageous for her family. But wasn't her mother skillful in business affairs? It certainly didn't surprise Maud. With the Deddes gone and the property divided up, everything would go downhill from there.

She thought of the radiant sunset, and of her missed walk along the river that was so green in the evenings and reflected the old elms of the Dior meadows. She could walk for hours in the valley, on the damp riverbanks, without getting tired of the strong odor of land and water and of the marsh where the waste of the summer was already rotting . . .

With her face in her pillow, she sobbed for a long time, her visage half-turned toward the window open to the western sky, already being deserted by the sun.

CHAPTER 18

ONE DAY SHE DECIDED TO VENTURE ALONG THE ROAD TO THE Pardal. June was coming to an end. The harvests were waiting for the reapers. Only the vines, spread out on the sides of the hills, were still turning green under the brilliant light, preferring the more tender and dreamy light of autumn to ripen.

The men were waiting in their cool houses to emerge once again in the full light of day, once summer had drawn to a close. Nothing troubled the torpor of their surroundings and of the countryside except, from time to time, the flowing shadow of a cloud passing by, very low and at an unusual speed, as if fleeing the disturbing calm of the sky.

Lovely rows of poplars alternated with small dark hedges of wild rosebushes, dividing the region into checkered patterns of gradated green, varying according to the direction the hills faced. Below, in the shadow of elms and alders that cast the noble hue of their pale foliage over the anonymous luxuriance of other trees, all uniformly dark, the Dior flowed quickly by . . .

Once outside, Maud didn't know what to do. She sat on an embankment and waited. Little by little she was seized by the same despair as in her room; she waited in vain for the end of the afternoon. Nobody passed by on the road, and evening came.

In the sky, a few clouds accumulated like fluffy sheep. There was no wind. Occasionally the lowing of a cow came from afar and gave Maud a start; filled with grass, tired of grazing, producing long, muffled ruminations, the animal was asking for its stable. Alone in the sky, the crows traced the irregular lines of their flight. Flying high, they broke the silence with their hoarse calls, vaguely announcing that angry times were coming, although it wasn't clear whose anger or against whom it was directed. Certainly, no people passed by.

The clay road was beige. Almost the whole expanse of the sky was also beige, a light beige hanging over Maud's head, thicker near the horizons close to the mud. Soon the birds also went to sleep; from time to time, one of them, uneasy with its location, would fly, worried, toward a neighboring bush.

A contrite dog headed home, slowly and wearily, like a human. As he passed by, he encountered Maud with his lifeless eyes, which made him look like a thing among other inert things.

The young woman set out again. Now the light that the sky poured onto the countryside no longer hurt her. Walking down the road, she looked back from time to time to take in all the scenery around her. Suddenly she found herself face-to-face with George Durieux.

She muffled a cry, because she hadn't expected him, while George, for his part, looked at her with great uncertainty.

In the gentle, subdued light, he took on an appearance that she didn't recognize. He had the bearing of a farmer and the stance of an animal ready for a fight. He wasn't doing anything, as usual, and his huge, useless strength got in the way of his breathing and his gestures.

"You were coming home? It's crazy, but you frightened me . . ." Composing herself, Maud smiled and put her hand flat against his chest. With this unexpected gesture she protected herself from the strange presence that broke into her solitude.

He was caught up at first in his emotions but then spoke roughly to her. "You were making off again, weren't you? Admit it . . ." She couldn't believe she had run into him; she thought he was at Semoic. What was he doing hanging around the house instead of coming in? And those knocks on the door? Had she been dreaming?

"No, I just came outside," she muttered. He looked disconcerted. She turned away somewhat so as not to look at him. "Come with me for a moment." He followed her, knowing, nevertheless, that he had been fooled and that she would soon be emboldened by her desertion.

They went in. While she closed the shutters, she heard him murmuring, "I love you, Maud. I've been so unlucky with you . . ." The servant had gone. Maud went to the kitchen to prepare drinks.

What did she want? He thought about the night below the shed, when she had set about looking for the iron bar with the same determination that now hardened her looks, chiseling a deep wrinkle into her forehead, so unusual on her face. He would never have come to her if he hadn't first met her on the path and been invited in. Now, however, because he had met her . . . Maybe she would stay, after all, for she never spoke about leaving; he never pushed her to decide one way or the other—in fact, it was just the opposite. Maybe, even though she wasn't happy, she had decided to stay. That was what he wanted—for her to decide on her own.

"Maud!" He called as loudly as if she had been very far from him. She guessed that he wanted her, and wanted her to come to him right away, feeling the return of his boldness and intoxicated with the dizziness his newfound confidence gave him . . .

She reappeared, carrying a tray full of drinks. He took it out of her hands, set it down randomly, and taking her by the shoulders, toppled her over onto a chair in front of him. She said nothing. A kind of curiosity made the gray of her eyes sparkle—a gray full of light, not like lifeless metal, but like mercury ready to flee, a gray that made gray the very color of passion. She let herself go with the natural, animal-like feebleness of the female who lends herself to male desire, even when she doesn't feel it spontaneously herself.

Usually when he came into the bedroom, he would slide toward her in the darkness, and it was she who would facilitate his pleasure. He would moan with terrible rage, and in those moments, she felt she was the strongest . . .

When he pushed her over onto the chair, she thought he was going to talk to her, but all he could do was repeat her name with a panting voice whose varied intonations expressed the cruel alternation of his despair and his love. She stayed immobile, her shoulder slightly raised, her hands open on her knees, while her lips slowly parted and a fine, shiny white blade appeared.

Suddenly he burst out laughing; what he didn't dare admit, he hid under this loud laugh: "When you leave, Maud, do you know what I'm going to do?" She didn't flinch. "Do you know what I'm going to do?"

Why did he evade all their moments of pleasure? She wouldn't understand until much later. Springing up, she grabbed his shoulder and gave him her mouth. But he broke away and exclaimed, "What do you want me to do? There won't be anything left for me to do, just like now, I'll be incapable of taking you back."

He kissed her, but almost without desire. Maud kept herself from giving him, even for an instant, the mad hope he desired. Lying can become such a common occurrence that a lie can escape from one's lips without one enduring any suffering as a consequence. But Maud was weak when it came to lying—even if she willed herself to do it, her words would have betrayed her.

Their joined lips were cold, but they preferred this contact to that of their eyes, which fled from each other . . . "Anyway, I don't care," mumbled George, "just as I don't care about suffering. When someone despises themselves as much as I do, it's perhaps the only thing that gives you a little dignity in your own eyes . . ."

She sank into his arms, and between his legs, sliding her head against his shoulder. His veins pounded heavily against her ear. She was sad, sadder than him, and felt only contempt for herself. Her took her, mechanically, for the last time.

He didn't even show up anymore for meals, which were served to Maud in her bedroom, and he inflicted on her from that point on the torment of absolute solitude. She felt dreadfully weary. Her tiredness grew from day to day; soon she could not eat the meals that the servant brought up to her and had to lie down for several hours at a time. George inquired as to what she wanted to eat; he thought she was bored and was showing her discouragement this way.

The old servant found her lying on her bed with a terrible paleness. "If you want, I'll tell monsieur you're not feeling well . . . ," she offered. Then, stopping herself, she became fearful—fearful that Maud would hang on to this master whom she adored. The servant lied, in a soft voice. "I think it's this heat," and then: "It's no kind of life staying shut up all day long . . ."

However, it was by virtue of the old woman's embarrassed look, of someone wanting to flee, that Maud understood she was pregnant.

CHAPTER 19

GEORGE SLEPT ON THE DINING ROOM COUCH AND LEFT FIRST thing every morning.

Maud hesitated. Should she tell him? Even if she no longer loved him the way she once had, he still had all her esteem. He would have married her if she had consented to it. The whole problem was with her, with her lack of will. Wasn't it unworthy of her to agree now to what she had refused?

Moreover, she still intended to leave. The idea that her family might have left frightened her. Her child was not yet detached enough from her life for it to count more than she did.

She was served her meals quite early, so that George wouldn't be home yet. The servant hid from her master that the dishes came back almost intact, so he stopped worrying. Maud's boredom finally reached such depths that the thought of her child no longer occupied her mind. As her doubt disappeared, she thought of it even less.

She stopped reading. The things she thought about had no

relationship to her present life. She became absorbed in memories that suddenly distinguished themselves from others, for no apparent reason, and took on the strange proportion of nightmares.

Very early one morning, she was awakened by repeated knocking on the door. George opened it; he said something she didn't understand. She jumped out of bed and got dressed in haste, not being able to hurry as much as she would have liked because her hands were cold and she was trembling. For three weeks she had been waiting, hidden away in this narrow room. And now it had happened: someone, abruptly, remembered her.

George called her with a strangled voice, and she noisily pushed open the bolt on the door, to show that she was up. As soon as she was dressed, she opened the shutters. The day was just beginning to break, turning the horizon green. Since the beginning of her exile she had lived off the vision of this landscape, but because she had never seen it at the crack of dawn, she didn't recognize it right away. She stopped a moment to look at it and then resolved to go downstairs.

In the dining room the awakening day entered by the open door, so indistinct one couldn't predict what kind of day it would be, while dark shadows still reigned in the far corners of the room. George had dressed hastily in an old pair of pants and a shirt pulled across his chest with a shiver. His messy brown hair gave him a rough-and-tumble look. Standing near the couch, he remained silent.

In front of him, Mrs. Taneran was seated. As usual, she wore a long black dress. A hat with a brim that was too large hid her face and somewhat crushed her silhouette. Beside her, on the ground, was a traveling bag. Without lifting her head, she said calmly, "So, are you coming down?"

On hearing her mother's forced voice, Maud imagined that her brothers were waiting behind the door, on the lookout for her appearance. The creaking of the stairs beneath her feet soon exasperated her. Her throat was as dry as if it had been made of stone.

Instinctively, she mustered her strength. The effort prevented her from seeing George, who was looking at her, and caused her to forget him.

Partially concealed by her big hat, Mrs. Taneran's features did not stand out the way they usually did. Her eyelids were swollen with sleep, and to avoid lifting her eyes to look at Maud and George, she focused on the ground. But her emotions could be guessed by the redness of her neck and the quiver of her pursed lips. She tried to control herself, but she was too old to hide an emotion inscribed on her bruised flesh that made her look even more pitiful.

Maud considered her mother a moment, then drew so close that Mrs. Taneran could not hold back a nervous gesture. Standing up, Maud's mother declared, "No, you've hurt me too much." Then, turning toward George, more embarrassed than she would have liked to appear, she continued. "You're going back to Bordeaux soon? I hope you will not prolong your holidays any longer . . ."

George gave a polite bow. "Don't worry, I'm leaving . . ." He might possibly have liked to say something to Maud, but he felt hindered by the presence of this older woman.

He accompanied them both to the doorway, and when they

were barely out, the door closed curtly. Maud perceived the noise of the latch. She thought she would come back some- day, at a time that would have nothing in common with what was happening now, a time of peace and sadness.

The night had not totally vanished; the countryside was without shadows and gently lit by a light arising in the east, from a gash in the sky and clouds. Mrs. Taneran announced, "It's four thirty. If we walk quickly, we'll get to the train for Bordeaux by six o'clock." To Maud's surprise, no one was waiting for them.

On each side of the lane, which was white with dryness, the tops of the cypress trees, of a faded green, moaned gen- tly in the breeze that lapped at them with little swigs. Maud walked behind her mother. As on the day she ran away, she was wearing nothing but a summer dress. She was cold. Mrs. Taneran didn't notice, absorbed as she was in her thoughts. "Your brothers are on the road, by the Pecresse house," she said shortly. "They're coming with us to Bordeaux. I have some errands to run there . . ."

Her tone was almost familiar, although she still feigned a refusal to look at her daughter. She walked quickly and Maud had to step up her pace. Then, automatically, she took her mother's traveling bag. At first, she felt a resistance, but her mother's fingers suddenly let go; their eyes met for a second; they still had nothing to say to each other, but by mutual agreement, they sped up a little. Behind them, clusters of dust rose and swirled for an instant. Leaving The Pardal on the right, they turned off onto the hollow road and passed along- side the Uderan grounds.

At that point Mrs. Taneran declared, "I've sold the property to the Pecresses, who will take it over as tenant farmers; it's a very good deal. I keep the majority of my rights. It would have been hard for me to let go of my precious house at my age . . . Fifty thousand francs," she exclaimed. "They gave me fifty thousand francs in cash. That's excellent, you know . . ."

Maud continued to walk with her head down, without responding. Her mother's indulgence astonished her. Without directly referring to their quarrel, her words erased it: "It doesn't seem to surprise you that I came looking for you . . ."

Maud murmured, "It was time that you came . . ."

Mrs. Taneran could barely hold back a sign of satisfaction. "That worked out well! I suspected you had had enough. Personally, I thought he was too old for you. I wanted to tell you— here people don't know you were staying with Durieux . . . You didn't go out, you were careful, that's good . . . The Pecresses know and have kept quiet. You will come to know them; they're good people . . . So, I was saying that . . . We've left to get you, you are coming from Auch, from your aunt's, Taneran's sister, do you hear? At whose place you have just spent a couple of weeks . . . Afterward, well afterward, you will have to accept what we tell you, because you have seriously compromised yourself . . ."

Mrs. Taneran blushed. "John Pecresse adores you; he'll overlook everything . . ."

It was extraordinary: Maud hadn't thought about that yet. Without waiting any longer, she opened up with what was tormenting her. "It's impossible, don't even think about it; I'm expecting a child."

Mrs. Taneran stopped, her eyes bloodshot, and looked at her daughter without seeing her; she pulled her hat off her head and threw it down; then, covering her eyes with her hands like someone seized by vertigo, she gropingly sought the embankment and collapsed. A minute went by, then two minutes, and Maud became fearful. The state of dejection she had lived in for weeks now brusquely stopped. She thought she saw frightening signs on her mother's face. Maud took her in her arms and began to kiss her dress and her arms, as if this explosion of love could pull her mother from an ending she suddenly found so appealing. But it was purely Maud's imagination, for Mrs. Taneran, having passed through a series of emotions in a few seconds, including terror, despair, and the desire to give up living, quickly recovered. She came back to reality, gently, strangely, the way sick people recover their health. She took Maud in her arms and then held her away from her and considered her with unspoken tenderness. And she forgot the role that she was supposed to play.

"Don't cry. I've just been suffering from dizzy spells lately. The blood rushes to my head and makes me suffocate . . . So, you're expecting a child? This marriage with John Pecresse, you can be sure it's not my idea . . . It's Jacques's. I know he did it for the good of all of us, but still it's been hard for me to accept . . . What could I have done? I knew you were at Durieux's place, but he never wanted me to go there for fear I would raise suspicions . . ."

She took a small breath before adding, "He's more cautious than I am, of course. Now what will become of us? I've already received and considerably dipped into the fifty thousand francs. Yes, I had to repay the furniture! And then Jacques had debts . . ."

She didn't stop caressing Maud, who wept like a fool; she

stroked her shoulders, her arms, her hair . . . "We're going back to Paris, don't worry! Durieux will come and get you. I'll come back here alone. For the moment, that's all there is to do." They set out again.

At the bend leading to the national highway, two silhouettes of the same height suddenly appeared. Maud recognized her brothers. They were losing patience. "You think it's funny to make us wait in these conditions . . . ," started Jacques.

His mother cut him off. She explained to her sons that they were going back to Paris. They accepted without trying to understand, happy to leave, exhausted from having gotten up so early in the morning. "We just have enough time," said Mrs. Taneran.

Maud began to walk on the left embankment, a little apart from the others. On the road, their footsteps rang out with a strange sound in the surrounding silence. Soon a crossroad appeared. There was a white cross and a sign: La Rayvre. Beyond it, the road sped down a steep slope.

PART III

CHAPTER 20

AT FIRST GLANCE, ONE MIGHT HAVE TAKEN THEM FOR ORDI-nary travelers coming home from holidays. They endured their private time together in silence. The joggling of the train soon put them to sleep in the confident, relaxed attitude of people who have had their fill of scenery for the year, and who only have eyes for their neighbors. When the Bordeaux train passed below Uderan, Maud and her mother barely gave a last glance at the house.

They didn't arrive until eleven o'clock at night at the Austerlitz station in Paris. It was a beautiful night. The taxi that took them home went up the rue des Écoles and the boulevard Saint-Michel, whose facades were all ablaze with lights. Maud, who was sitting on the fold-up seat, noticed her older brother's look of false annoyance. As they approached a large café, he knocked on the partition and stopped the car. It was then that their first argument broke out, partially obscured by the noise of passing cars, and shortened by the implacable ticking of the meter.

"Stop, taxi." The shock was so unexpected that Mrs. Taneran was thrown toward the front by the brakes. Her mouth puffed up as if to say something, but no sound, no word, was able to come out. Jacques had already placed his foot on the running board. He acted as if he were getting out but then turned back toward his mother, and with a quick word, in the style of a consummate con artist, asked, "Do you have a thousand francs? I won't be home late . . ."

Maud preferred to look elsewhere, for example, at the café whose light shone right into the taxi. As always in these cases, her nerves tightened, and she breathed with more and more difficulty as the oppression grew. Time stood still for a moment, ebbing with the slowness of a nightmare. Mrs. Taneran was debating within herself. In the crimson light, she appeared to be crying. "Sometimes you just don't think! On the very night of our arrival!"

She repeated, "No, no," getting up partway from her seat, then falling back down. Her big black hat had hit the roof of the car; she held it in one hand and straightened it with the other. On this particular night, the hat gave her a look of ridiculous solemnity.

Jacques's voice was barely audible, but scathing. He whispered again, "I'm telling you to give me a thousand francs . . ., at least a thousand francs." His hand reached out in the dark, like a beggar. Mrs. Taneran articulated several "nos," as well as words like "forget it" and "it's no use insisting," phrases that revealed more and more panic and became less and less convincing. Her short sentences fell to the ground.

"You just took in fifty thousand francs, and you refuse to give me a bill? Is that it?" He had almost yelled, but without compromising himself, without drawing the attention of the taxi driver, who didn't even turn around. His silent cry and its veiled threat had a great impact on the Taneran family circle. Mrs. Taneran stopped quibbling and reminded him right away, with a seared voice, "You're not the only one in the family . . ."

Henry Taneran joined in, daring to budge a little in the back of the car by rolling his distraught eyes as if he were asking for help. Jacques continued methodically. "And you think that's how it's going to be?" he insisted. "I accepted, or rather we accepted, Henry and I, that you bring her back"—he pointed at Maud—"and now you're treating us on the same level as her? What's that supposed to mean?" Henry hesitated to join in with his brother, who kept repeating like a refrain, "And you think that's how it's going to be?"

The scene didn't last more than two minutes. The click of Mrs. Taneran's old purse could be heard. A hand stretched itself out, then disdainfully crumpled the bills and pocketed them. Soon Jacques was no more than an elegant silhouette disappearing into the night light, his right hand thrust into the pocket of his jacket . . .

The driver turned around at last, and it was Maud who reminded him of the address. In front of her, her mother squirmed about like a madwoman, talking to herself and struggling against a danger that she alone seemed to perceive. Her hardened voice broke from time to time, turning into a sob of helplessness that left her eyes dry. "You won't end up with a thing, did you hear me, not a thing. And I'll leave for elsewhere . . . Oh! I'm an unlucky mother . . ."

Maud, leaning toward the front, gazed at the small halo of

light that preceded the car. Henry, sitting beside Mrs. Taneran, took on his usual attitude in these cases: an exasperated look. The rest of the trip was calmer. Mrs. Taneran became attentive to the moving of the taxi again. She recovered little by little from her emotions as they got closer and closer to home. Besides, the children always kept from bringing up again any of the words she spoke in such moments. They felt a certain mistrust for her fits of anger, which they found cowardly, because her outbursts came only after the danger had passed.

Maud noticed she hadn't been targeted in this flood of reproach. Her mother always avoided speaking about any of her children in particular.

In braking, the taxi skidded on the slope of the street. The noise woke up the concierge. When Mrs. Taneran went by the concierge's apartment, the woman, still half-asleep, poked her head out. "Oh! It's you? People have come by several times looking for Mr. Jacques." Mrs. Taneran approached her; she had regained her friendly look. The other woman hesitated and then spoke: "Yes, the police . . . Oh! I'm sure it's nothing . . ."

Mrs. Taneran stopped, seized with emotion. "Oh, my Lord," she said. Then she caught herself and tried to explain: "Of course, who else could it be?" She had the force of will to resist leaving the concierge too rapidly, while the other woman desperately stretched out her neck in order to learn something more.

The five flights were hard to climb. Henry and Maud followed their mother, whose shortness of breath betrayed her exhaustion. From time to time she stopped and turned toward

Henry. "Do you know what that means? It's certainly connected with the Tavares Bank . . ."

Henry refused to respond to anything. He lowered his head and tightened his mouth, and his eyes fled the gaze of his family; he had the kind of closed look of which people say, "You won't get anything out of him." And, in truth, whatever happened in his family, Henry Taneran proudly acted as if he were a disinterested party. The pleasure he took when people asked for his advice was such that he made it last right up to the limits of their patience.

Old Mr. Taneran appeared in the doorway, wrapped in a flannel bathrobe. No one had warned him of his family's arrival, and he seemed quite surprised. Mrs. Taneran didn't even give him time to open his mouth. "What's this story about the police? The concierge doesn't seem to know . . ."

"Unfortunately, I didn't try to find out either. Your son's affairs don't concern me . . . How are you doing?"

His words came out so naturally that he must have prepared them in advance. His wife stretched out her ravaged face to him. He rubbed her cheeks against his unshaven cheeks as he embraced her, and did the same for Maud and Henry. Then he grabbed the suitcases his wife was carrying and set them down.

"Thank you," she said. "I certainly thought of writing you, my dear Taneran, but I had to sell the property. I had your authorization with me, you know. A good sale? Yes. But couldn't I wait until tomorrow to talk about it?" She dropped into a chair and removed her hat. "You really don't know anything?"

"My dear wife . . ."

She stopped him with a gesture and added softly, "Every-thing's okay?"

"Yes, thank you. I spent my whole time working, and you know that I like my work. However, I decided to leave for Auch in July this year. My dear, it certainly looks as if we will never take our holidays together. I'm so sorry . . ."

Almost at the same time, they said, "See you tomorrow," and then he withdrew.

By the looks she was sending their way, her children under-stood that she was sinking little by little into a deep pit of anxiety. As he fled her, Henry was the first to say in an uncer-tain voice, "It can't be much. Don't get so upset . . ."

Maud sat down along the wall of the dining room, facing her mother. The bags were strewn in the middle of the room. Henry came and went, from one room to another . . .

Mrs. Taneran looked at her daughter with empty eyes. She didn't say anything, aware that her children couldn't calm her down. At a certain point, however, she thought she knew the answer and cried out, "Henry, it's that woman, surely, if it's not about the Tavares Bank . . ."

"Are you crazy! That's over," responded Henry from his room.

Mrs. Taneran shook her head and sank back into scratching her brain for an answer. She plunged silently into terrifying hypotheses, surfacing with difficulty, but feeling more reas-sured about things. Maud was thinking, "The police?" How easy it was for her to imagine Jacques between two agents, with a face that reminded her of the one he had worn a cer-tain night at the inn.

It was a face disfigured by fear and on which shame was

perhaps still written, in small, pale patches around his eyes and mouth—one that could be Jacques's at the time of his death. A face feebly dangling above true sadness and bringing back for the first time his childhood face—a childhood emerging at last and stunned by death's proximity. All that emanated from this face—the undying vanity, the perpetual lament arising from his pleasure-seeking, and an ugliness enveloped in beauty—would one day be shattered.

CHAPTER 21

"MAUD, GO TO BED."

Mrs. Taneran wanted to wait for the return of her son alone. The look on her daughter's face didn't bode well. "I know you all detest each other. You're never happier than when misfortune strikes one of the others. Now that it's about saving him . . . If I wasn't there, poor boy!" She went from anger to worry, like someone who suffers and seeks the position in which she will suffer the least.

"They're going to take him away. You'll see that they came to take him away." She moaned, sometimes like a little girl, sometimes in the tragic way of a mother who is trembling for one of her own . . . "Nothing will have been spared me in this life, nothing. What's going to happen, Maud?"

"Mother, it's all the same to me."

"I know, dear. You unfortunately have other things to think about." Her mother was so used to her worries that only the most urgent ones counted for her. The others, with more distant deadlines, allowed one to breathe a little before envisioning them.

Maud approached her mother. She hadn't kissed her since the morning. In the train, they avoided each other because of Jacques and Henry. Mrs. Taneran began to stroke her daughter's head. Her fingers, a little numb, sank into her hair, lifting up the smooth, shiny mass. Her hand played with her round forehead, the slightly receding chin, and the broad cheeks of her child, while her anxious mind did not settle down. "You don't know him, Maud, but at heart he's a good boy. With me I would even say that he's the nicest of the three of you, the most attentive . . ."

The naïveté of her mother always astonished her. But her mother's caresses felt good on Maud's face. After being deprived of her mother's attention for so long, she welcomed it like a spring breeze. "He may be very likable, Mother. That congeniality hides him from you. But he's so rotten that he's as light as a branch of deadwood . . ."

Mrs. Taneran's hand stopped instantly. They separated, with each one maintaining her position. And Maud, brutally, felt that she became the prey of an unnamed despair, in which this woman forever rejected her.

Mrs. Taneran shuddered. Was it possible to pronounce such a judgment so coldly? She, the mother, could suffer. But her illusions remained, despite her grief, indefinitely. It was because she believed in her son that she lived in a dream-world, inaccessible to any contradictions of reality.

At certain moments, she hated Maud. Brutally, this child disfigured the object of her love. And what remained for Mrs. Taneran in confronting this particular form of suffering, without the freshness of her faith? "Be quiet—aren't you ashamed? Just think of the fact that someone could come and take him away tomorrow. That dirty Tavares, that filthy toad . . ."

"If Jacques left Paris for a time," Maud shot back, "it was surely because of this business. You thought it was something else, just like us, didn't you? That he was weeping for his wife, that he was going to mourn for her in the country?"

All perceptiveness concerning her son embarrassed Mrs. Taneran. As the mother, she saw what was true, she saw with adorable grace his times of abandonment, even his most obvious weaknesses. "What can I say! I have no idea. It's perhaps somewhat for the Tavares affair, and a little for everything . . ." Only she could find reasons to keep on loving him, to prefer him to the others.

"By the way, Mother, if he wanted to marry me to Pecresse, he'll still want to do it; don't you think he'll arrange it when he finds out the state I'm in, so as not to lose the benefits of your deal with the Pecresses?"

"You'd best be quiet, Maud. You're able to say such harsh things that sometimes I doubt your goodness. When your brother hears that you're expecting Durieux's child, he'll be the first to give you good advice, do you hear . . . ?"

Maud kept quiet. George's house passed before her eyes, sad and tranquil, open to the countryside. The yew trees swayed in front of the windows, and in the distance one could see the Uderan pine forest. Little by little the daylight disappeared. One by one the crickets sang their hearts out. Up above, at L'Oustaou, the velvety moles were adventuring toward the pine forest, full of fear. George didn't come in. It felt as if he were prowling around the house. They had separated for reasons that were difficult for her to understand. But Maud suddenly thought it would be easier now for her to live with George.

The ceiling light brutally lit up the room, in which the luggage was still strewn on the furniture and the floor. No noise was coming from the back rooms, where Henry slept, and old Taneran snored in the adjoining room. Everything seemed calm and the same as usual.

Why then was Maud crying for once? Her child's tears wrongly reassured Mrs. Taneran. Wasn't she crying because of remorse? She had truly been shaken up. Her daughter's words reminded her mother of the misery of her own life. Even if she spoke of it often, Mrs. Taneran rarely felt it in all its depth. She, too, wept, but softly, already as an old woman would.

At last she spoke to Maud. "You'll be happy with Durieux. Why say such ridiculous things to me? You see that you regret them afterward. You know I'll miss you . . . Obviously, my life is not happy. A mother's duty is always toward the most unfortunate of her children, the one everyone else abandons . . ."

CHAPTER 22

MAUD WENT TO BED, BUT SHE COULDN'T SLEEP THAT NIGHT. Her mother had calmed down a little. She came and went, unpacking the suitcases, rummaging through them. From time to time she tiptoed into the room, opened up the closet, went through things, and put things away. Tireless, Mrs. Taneran continued to circulate mysteriously throughout the house, coming back once again. They were so used to her nighttime goings-on that they didn't bother anybody. Maud listened to her; each of her movements in the silence of the house took on the specific merits of patience and unrelenting fervor. Maud felt alone and had nothing more to hope for than what she already knew.

Soon she would return to Uderan and would get married. Then she would leave for Bordeaux with George. She wouldn't come back to Uderan until the holidays, and that was certainly enough, given that the Pecresses' hatred of them and the farmers' disdain for them would always be simmering beneath the surface. George worked with his father and led an inconsistent life, sometimes steady, sometimes debauched. She didn't clearly see what place she would have in his existence. Her life had begun at the exact moment she had spoken to her mother and had gained the certainty that no other solution would present itself for such a clearly defined situation.

Maybe George was already waiting for her. When they had separated in the morning, he had appeared calm and almost satisfied. Probably they didn't love each other anymore. She blushed at the idea of going back, of forcing him to take her back. How could she dare to appear before his eyes? She couldn't stay here, though. Her mother had chosen to leave her, and the separation had already happened in her heart. She had understood this in hearing her mother's gentle, sympathetic voice this evening.

No doubt she would leave as soon as this week—the sooner the better. At any rate, the time she spent here would be useless.

If Jacques had not existed, perhaps her mother would have kept her. In any case, she wouldn't have abandoned her so quickly, with this sort of unconscious relief. Without realizing it, Mrs. Taneran continued to create a vacuum around her older son and would do so right up until the time when only he would remain to receive the fullness of her love, once her duty had been fulfilled toward the others.

Maud wasn't upset with her mother; it was to her older brother that her thoughts kept returning. He was the one her hatred surrounded and whom she would have liked to be able to suffocate from a distance. She felt him pressed up against her, destiny against destiny. They were as closely linked as two victims, entangled together. Yet she couldn't do anything. In terms of all the evil he had done, she felt it as much as if she had done it herself.

He had chased her, and misfortune had come to her. Perhaps, for his part, he had wished for it, like his mother, who for weeks hadn't shown any sign of life and had contrived with him to leave Maud alone.

The idea of her brother created a strange hurt, not exactly painful, but intolerable—a hurt she felt beating inside of her like an abscess.

So, he would have been assured of a life annuity from Uderan? That Pecresse would have provided for him? Mother, crazily, would have let him do it . . . It was possible . . .

How weak her mother was! There it was: she saw clearly what her mother had become, a creature without any strength, gifted with an illusory will that could be broken like a nutshell. Nothing. And it was Jacques who, day after day, had reduced his mother to nothing.

Since a very young age, Maud had imagined him as nasty, but in an instinctive and childish way, not more. Now she understood that it wasn't about a natural tendency such as courage or devotion. Jacques was mean as a sort of reverse action against himself. Doing good discouraged him in advance, and he carefully avoided it. He didn't dare try to be better, because every beginning, even that of an attitude, is arid and desolate like the break of day.

Thus, he found it preferable to sink little by little into meanness, and to deliver a more decisive blow each day to Taneran, Maud, and his mother, whom he held well in hand. His life took on unity and strength. He won victories; he got stronger. That's why every happy scene saddened him. Just thinking about it sent chills down Maud's spine . . .

The sound of the doorbell drew Maud from her numbness. Her mother's footsteps headed toward the door. Maud strained to hear. A kind of curiosity and also hope made her sit up in bed . . . Her mother was going to speak to him. Perhaps it was the beginning of a catastrophe so serious, so horrible, that it would eclipse everything else for a certain time . . . Crazy, she was crazy to believe it, or even anticipate such a windfall.

Her brother's resounding voice echoed in the hallway. When he came in, he always woke up everyone and didn't show any qualms about it. On the other hand, when he was sleeping, what perfect calm was maintained around him!

It was true; this voice drew her back into the past. It announced the same dreaded hours approaching dawn every night. Jacques boomed at his mother. "You're not in bed, what's the matter with you?"

"Be quiet," she pleaded. "I'm begging you to be quiet. The police were here for you while we were away . . ."

He was silent and then replied, "What are you talking about?"

Mrs. Taneran repeated what she had just said. Jacques must have been drinking, because his voice was sticky and he articulated slowly, like someone waking up. Soon Maud didn't hear them anymore. Maybe they were talking very, very quietly . . . And then Jacques went at it again, with sudden brutality: "Oh! They came? When? How many times? For heaven's sake, talk!"

"It's up to you to tell me, my dear . . ."

"It's Tavares," he replied. "I just need to play dead."

"You signed?" queried his mother. "For how much?"

"Fifty thousand," retorted Jacques, "but I'm telling you I

just need to play dead. They won't get me for a few loan pay-ments . . . Besides, it's old business, you remember . . ."

Maud fell back onto her bed. At the tone of her broth-er's voice, she understood there was no real danger. Noth-ing bizarre, nothing. Only Tavares, and with him, she knew, there was always a way to work things out. Life would take on its infernal ebb and flow.

They had entered the dining room. From time to time she picked up bits of sentences, like, "So you've finished cry-ing?" and then, "Oh, I was so fearful, my dear. Why did you do that?"

"It was for Muriel. I wanted to come to you, but surely you know me by now. I would have died rather than ask you for money. What can I do, I'm just like that!" Little by little he perked up again and held his head higher.

Maud deeply resented the filth of each of his words. Just the effect of his voice made her feel altered. She hadn't heard him for a long time, but he was still at the same place: he was still using his same old lies and pathetic exaggerations.

He was playing a new role in the eyes of his mother and Maud found he had increased in boldness and strength. Oh, what a show-off he was!

"I'm a fellow people don't really understand. Of course, I'm not talking about you! I've always said, 'You're a saint.' But them . . ."

"What are you planning to do?"

"Obviously, it would be better to pay . . . I'm not a crook. Fake papers, that's basically not my strong suit. I was recom-mended to the bank as Muriel's husband . . ."

He smelled the fifty thousand francs received the day before from the Pecresses that his mother had in her possession. "She won't say anything," thought Maud, "she won't tell him they don't have anything now on account of me . . ." And effectively, Mrs. Taneran let him go through all his useless tactics of cozying up to her. Perhaps she herself forgot that she owed this money to the Pecresses, if Maud wasn't going to marry John.

"Obviously, I was saying, it's better that I pay . . . I'll go back to work, and I'll pay. It'll take me ten years, but I'll get there . . ."

At the same time, his mother persisted in not offering anything. One had to really not know her (and he knew her well) to think she would decide from the outset not to give back the sum to the Pecresses. But Mrs. Taneran would let things unfold on their own until she came to a point of no return.

"It's not the first time something like this has happened," Jacques continued. "If you only knew how many times I've spared you from something like this you'd be amazed, my dear mother, amazed . . ."

And certainly, she would never be so naïve as to offer him what he wanted today. But one night, between them, and just between them, she would brusquely take the money from her closet, between two piles of sheets, and give it to him without saying a word. The passing days would have weakened their memory of the Pecresses, whose image was already fading. As for the Grants, they lived in reality.

Right up until dawn they talked together like that, softly. Mrs. Taneran let herself be beguiled, basically happy with these confidences that brought her closer to her son.

Maud didn't sleep. She didn't listen, either. She waited for the morning in order to leave. As soon as the first rays of dawn caused the night to fade, she got up. Then, not knowing what to do, she stayed glued to the middle of her room. She realized that before her departure for Uderan something was going to happen.

Already that something was inside her, in her mind, which little by little got used to it and let it take shape. Then she felt it on the outside, very small but living and focused and looking at her like the eye of a motionless bird.

The door of the dining room opened. Jacques said to his mother as he yawned, "They're sleeping. By the way, it's better not to tell anything to them or the old man. And especially not to my sister. You can say whatever you want about her; I know what I think about her now. I know women. Happily, she's going to be on her way . . ." They went toward the kitchen.

"Come," said the mother, "I'm not going to go to bed now, it's too late. I'm going to make a little coffee."

Maud slipped into the kitchen before them and waited. As soon as they saw her, they stopped in their tracks in the doorway. They didn't dare enter, held back by a vague fear. Mrs. Taneran tried to smile. "Are you crazy, my dear? What are you doing there?"

Jacques advanced very decidedly, pale and seized abruptly by anger that deformed his face. "What are you doing there? Let me at her, Mother . . ."

In truth, Maud didn't know what she was doing there. She only guessed that she irritated Jacques, in all her weakness, in all her distress simply presented, to the point of stirring up in him a desire for murder: the way one wants to kill an inoffensive animal after having wounded it, without thinking, without hatred. She looked at her brother, so pale in the early morning light, blown up with anger. He was looking around him for something he could use to crush his sister's face.

"You were spying on us, weren't you? Oh, you're lucky I'm holding myself back!" He lowered his arm slowly, with difficulty, in a gesture that showed how much he suffered for not having hit her.

Mrs. Taneran stammered a few words incoherently. She blushed, obviously ashamed at having been caught with her son in an intimate moment of complicity. Ah! That Maud! Wasn't it enough that she was pregnant, yes, illegitimately pregnant! . . . How unjust, when for once she had had a bit of happiness! Mrs. Taneran yelled, "Go to bed, do you hear me? You're a piece of dirt, a piece of dirt! Give that chair to your brother . . . "

In the next room, they could hear Henry stretching and yawning. Maud got up and gave the chair to her brother. Next, she turned around, feeling lighter . . .

And they barely heard the noise of the entrance door, which she closed behind her with great care.

CHAPTER 23

THE PASSERSBY BEGAN TO CRISSCROSS THE ROADS; THEY looked rested and walked briskly. In the heavily populated neighborhood of Clamart, which rises early, the cafés were already opening. The customers, almost all men—factory workers—jostled one another at the counter in front of their hot coffee. They came out with cigarettes hanging from their mouths, joking around with one another on the almost empty streets, and looking happy to breathe in the fresh morning air that didn't yet reek of the tiredness of the day.

In the lower part of town, which gave the impression of painful insomnia, the Seine flowed by. From place to place, the morning light filtered through the mist and cast a shimmering light on its green waters.

Although she hadn't slept, Maud felt nearly herself. She wrapped around her the coat she had grabbed in haste and began walking quickly. The slightly pungent wind snapped from time to time like a sea breeze and took away her breath. She walked faster and faster, like someone who is sustained or lifted up by some kind of hope, or caught up in a pleasant thought, with a forgotten smile fastened to her lips and her eyes blurred . . .

But soon she felt hungry and she tottered. Her empty head was filled with a harsh ringing noise, and her legs carried her as feebly as if she had been walking on the bridge of a boat. She had experienced this sensation for some time. She entered a café and drank a coffee with cream. She gently inhaled the odor, her arms leaning on the damp counter, and each sip made her feel a bit more comforted. The air in the café was humid and acidic, and saturated with human breath.

Soon Maud felt better and ordered another coffee. Customers were continuously coming and going. As they brushed by her, they stared and judged her. When she raised her eyes, she met their gazes, some simply curious, others already emboldened. A kind of irritation seized her. She stared at them in turn with an impertinence that was supposed to be courageous but only looked ridiculous.

"Dogs," she said to herself, "they're dogs; they're not going to leave me alone . . ." The men noticed her look and shrugged their shoulders. She calmed down after that and felt embarrassed . . . She went out.

It was then that the day appeared to return to its true worth, stretched out between empty hours. If she had a task to accomplish, it would take her at most a few minutes. But what would become of her until then? And yet it seemed impossible for her to imagine acting any differently. She thought of nothing and no one except the agonizing abyss of the day into which she was slowly plunging, and which seemed to close in over her like the sea over a living shipwreck, too slow to die or reach the bottom.

However, she had already experienced empty days, from

winter days with few hours of light, to those spent in her room at Uderan, contemplating without really seeing the summer landscape swollen with heat. But today didn't resemble any other; it was too resistant, too deep, too long to journey through.

As time went by, she found herself more and more alone, ever farther from the familiar shores of her life. The thing she had to do gradually took on more importance, without becoming bigger, and became more and more precise, while around her everything became vague and blurred and disappeared, as Maud found herself alone with it . . .

This vision didn't stay with her. Both annoying and tempting at the same time, it was no different than Maud herself. It was not exactly like a mirror, in which she couldn't have avoided seeing herself, but rather the very image of her solitude—a mirror over which she leaned, knowing only that she should have seen herself there, that she was there . . . without seeing herself.

Soon there was nothing but the two of them, this image and herself, in the immense sadness of the world. Maud knew that the only way to have done with the day and everything else was to do the thing she had in mind, which presented itself to her with more and more urgency. But, through sheer fear, she didn't yet dare to break this last mooring cable.

She walked quickly and soon had covered quite a distance along the route her mother used to take her sometimes on Sundays. Today the idle strollers were missing; in thinking back, Maud no longer recognized herself in the little girl who walked, tired and dreamy, beside Mrs. Taneran.

Clamart was already distant, although looking over her

shoulder she could make out the huge white hulk of the building in which they lived. Fog enveloped it, and the different floors could not be distinguished one from another. "As soon as I reach the woods of Meudon," she told herself, "I'll come back toward Paris. And while I'm waiting, I'll go to our neighborhood."

She killed time as best she could, continually fascinated by the thing she had to do, but not yet feeling resolved enough to do it outright, shamelessly. Patiently, she let herself be vanquished. She was waiting for the idea that had seized her, and to whose power of suggestion she was confusingly subjected, to come about on its own.

At the edge of the Meudon forest, she avoided going into the shadows cast by the trees and turned back. The lunch hour had passed, and people were returning to work. All at once, Maud found herself in an abandoned garden, which looked to her to be public, on account of the number of children playing there. She sat down for a moment. She thought about lunch. She had some money in her purse, but after starting out toward a restaurant, she came back to the garden, finding it unnecessary to eat.

A freshness fell from the foliage of the chestnut leaves. No one passed by in front of her, and from the bench where she was sitting, at the corner of the garden, she followed the boisterous movements of the children who were running around, stirring up visions of astonishing lightness. The world was in its place, diverse, immense.

Back home, life was probably continuing on as usual. They ate late. Right now, her brothers were snoring, and her mother was busy, lovingly preparing a meal. At noon hour she would say simply, "Let's sit down at the table without that crazy girl . . ." If Mrs. Taneran was a little worried, her worry was only on the surface. This dirty business with the Tavares Bank was at most a question of money. At worst, she would be obliged to appropriate the sum of money paid by the Pecresses. If they found fault with that, she would come to a private agreement with them. She would know how to handle them. At any rate, the whole thing would be put off until later.

All of that wasn't worth her slowing down the sacrosanct schedule of the day. As for forgery, she had confidence in her son. Her son could not do anything really wrong. He could deceive people, of course, and appear odious in the eyes of some . . . So what! She laughed it off—she, his mother, knew that all of that was only filthy foam floating on pure water, on the delightful nature of her child.

"He's a fake, of course," she must have said to herself, "but he's my son. He has reasons for not hesitating to do what he did." She felt strong and peaceful, as in the early days of her maternity. Life was going just fine.

In the shade, Maud gently reflected on the thing that wouldn't leave her. She thought about the mother of her childhood, her childhood with its soft gray eyes. And this woman still showed her gentleness. Oh, what a vile deed she was going to carry out against her, what a nasty job, indeed! She tried not to think about it. "When Jacques leaves, Mother will die of grief."

She couldn't do anything about it. *Her* mother had died the night before. She could envision her mother in the future, wrapped up in the memory of her absent son, alone with old

Taneran. Maybe at that moment she would expect some tenderness from her daughter. Mrs. Taneran would be exalted by misfortune, lost in a final illusion about her son.

Around three o'clock, Maud went back to her neighborhood, as she had promised herself she would do, but avoided crossing Clamart. The detour she obliged herself to take would be long, but her legs would have taken her even farther, if only she had been able to escape the infernal circle drawn around her by her idea. Little by little, walking very quickly, she lost sight of her family, as well as her reasons for sacrificing them forever. In one go, retracing her footsteps, she arrived at the police station of Clamart.

All of a sudden, she found herself in front of the clerk of the police station, standing still and feeling stupid, encumbered by her own body, whose weight was no longer lightened by the walk. And immediately she had the impression that the *thing* substituted itself for her.

"You have come to our place several times, regarding my brother Jacques Grant," she declared in a firm voice. "It's about the Tavares Bank. Well! I've come to tell you he's back . . ."

The clerk appeared surprised. He went toward the cupboard and pulled out a yellow file. Maud would have liked to leave. He said to her in a haughty voice, "Wait a minute, I'll take a look . . ." One minute, three minutes, five minutes, went by while the man consulted his file. Maud stood near him, her mind a blank.

Then something pitiful happened: after a moment, the man lifted his head and looked at the young woman without saying anything, as if he questioned her mental state. "I don't know what you're talking about," he said at last. "We went to your place, it's true. The Tavares Bank where your brother did business was a gang of crooks. Because we found his name, we went looking for him. At the same time, we suspected his complicity. But actually, he was the one who was robbed. He should have lodged a complaint. I don't see what you've come here for . . ."

At the sense of relief she felt, Maud realized how afraid she had just been. When she went out, her legs could hardly carry her. With difficulty, she headed toward a small square, where she sat down on a bench.

She knew this place, not far from home, very well; on one side was a pharmacy, and on the other, a little Protestant church surrounded by a well-tended garden and nicely trimmed shrubs; the church was made of wood; its porch was topped by a frieze of veneered wood and decorated with openwork on which a Latin inscription was displayed in gold letters. The wall of a public school constituted the third side of the square. There were no children going in or out. The church door, as well, remained closed.

It was very chilly and the benches were empty. From time to time, Maud became physically aware of the cold. She remained motionless as much as possible because the slightest gesture sent shivers up her back. Besides, her walk had tired her out so much that she didn't feel the need to make the slightest movement. She barely felt the rhythm of her respiration, which regularly broke through the stuffiness of her chest with a fresh breath.

She had nothing more to think about in regard to what had just come to such an abrupt end. She had reached, all at once, a definitive point of no return. It stopped being an issue in her mind, unless she forced herself to think about it.

Little by little, evening came. She remembered having seen it through Durieux's window, day after day, rising from the horizon, slowly thickening the thin line of the Dior. Shades of gray and mauve and sometimes a brilliant strawberry red blended and mixed together, before all slipping into a humid grayness. Soon the countryside could hardly be distinguished, except for the bright line of the river. It was then that the powerful and radiant night tide rose, swollen with vapor. Odors rose from the plowed fields, the bushes, the clover fields, the vegetable gardens. There were walnuts not far from the house, and the scent reached Maud, glazed and intensely bitter. It was the moment when she feared standing out too vividly on the luminous backdrop of the window, which she closed with regret.

Oh yes, she certainly remembered. Her misfortune was undoubtedly enormous. She considered it without sadness and even with a kind of satisfaction. It stretched out around her, much more imposingly now than when it was right then and there—a vast region over which she had reigned.

She had done what was important. Jacques's fate no longer depended on her will—she couldn't do anything about it! Her mind stood still at the certainty she now had, like a serpent coiled up around itself.

Intermittently people entered the pharmacy, whose door opened with the ringing of a bell. Soon the window was intensely lit up. Time passed, and it felt good to let it go by without expecting anything from it.

However, Maud soon felt a malaise that sharpened quickly until it became painful . . . she was hungry. The sensation soon became very unpleasant. The memory of her child came back to her. It was quite strange but reassuring that this distant phantom was always near her in spite of her life's worst vicissitudes.

What an idea, all the same, to denounce her brother. Preposterous! In reality, Jacques had been cheated by Tavares! . . . She tried in vain to hold on to her hatred, but the reasons she had given herself slid from her mind like sand running through her fingers.

The police scared Jacques. "What a joke!" she thought. And her mother, who was so upset! It wouldn't have taken much for her to laugh out loud. What cowards, what insignificant little nobodies who didn't even keep their crooked promises: her family!

Her torment vanished altogether. It got dark, slowly at first, as the light died down, and then brutally, with a blackness that spread and stretched out over them. Night was no longer something far away and impalpable, but something that brushed up against her skin, like the presence of a huge, peaceful beast that wanted to lick her. She felt the shadow inside herself, too, filling her throat and almost stopping her from breathing.

Tomorrow she would write, or else her mother would do it. Next, she would wait for George's reply, or that might not even be necessary. Shame had disappeared from her conscience. It was time for her to go—to leave them behind.

In reality, she wasn't going away feeling good about it,

but feeling, instead, a sense of curiosity. How would George appear to her, now that she was going to belong to him?

Maud got up and decided to go home, reasonably. The day now stretched out behind her, like a mountain she had climbed and come back down. She walked calmly in the dark, without feeling any other burdens inside except that of the child she was carrying.

.

CHAPTER 24

THREE DAYS AFTER MAUD'S DEPARTURE FROM HIS HOME, George received a letter from Mrs. Taneran.

Sir,

On the back of the envelope you have read my name. And perhaps you have already guessed why, before I go any further.

The few times I saw you were enough to give me a good picture of you. I address the friend you could have been and which you were not as a result of circumstances as disagreeable as they were unexpected. Believe me, sir, my own liking for you was no less than that of my older son. Right from the beginning of our relationship, Jacques hoped, in fact, that it would last and go beyond the narrow and occasional scope of the holidays. That is why, in regard to his sister, he resorted to making up a small tale about John Pecresse. He hopes you will not hold it against him.

A rare insight, and the constant concern about family interests that have always kept Jacques in a state of tension, pushed him to distance his sister from you, to keep this child from the company of a man who was to exercise an extraordinary power of seduction over her. He only succeeded, unfortunately, in slowing down the arrival of the greatest misfortune that has ever happened to me. If I had listened to him from the beginning, I might have avoided this catastrophe, but you know, a mother is always blind, especially when she isn't supported by a father's firm attitude. Even though her whole life is comprised of love for her children, she makes mistakes . . .

Do I need to elaborate on such a subject? You know my daughter well enough to discern in her a tenacity that is all the more dangerous because it rarely makes itself known: you have been the happy object of her choice.

The solitude and specific atmosphere in which she grew up are the causes of her uncommunicative and violent nature (in which the worst temptations can smolder because there is nothing to provide a distraction from them). All this has come about, even though my son and I have never stopped correcting her natural tendencies with great severity. Until she met you, these tendencies lay dormant and dangerously turned inward, in a reserve and timidity that should have frightened us even more. In a family that has had no previous incidents as shameful as this, nothing else could explain such a catastrophe.

I hope, sir, that through the gentle bliss of a situation in which her nature will finally blossom in plain view, you will be rewarded for your goodness.

Maud will arrive at Semoic Friday night on the 9:40 train. She will have some luggage, so perhaps you should send someone to the train station. I will not belabor the reasons for this sad return . . .

I know that my daughter is heartbroken at the idea of leaving me, even though her sadness doesn't show. She will suffer a lot from our separation. She is a poor child who is not lacking in intelligence and fully accepts the severity of her punishment.

I cannot go back to Uderan to accompany her. I would advise you not to stay there too long and not to celebrate your marriage there. Once time has accomplished its work, I will come back one day to sort out a situation that has been much overblown.

I fear you may be mistaken about my feelings. In your eyes I probably don't respond as I should to the love of a child who adores me. Make no mistake about it: I love her with a tenderness that is so strong and so poignant that I do not dare to broach the subject. There are loves one can never get over, even between a mother and her child, loves that should be lived exclusively. As you know, I am the mother of more than one fatherless child.

There is nothing more for me to say except to wish you happiness. Late engagements can often be marvelous, believe me.

Receive my child, my dear child, with whom the abruptness, the gentleness, and the fragrance of childhood depart from my house. Warm her with the approach of fall, when even nature is sad. I owe myself to this task that is as difficult as it is inept, since it will come to an end with me.

Thank you. I will see you both again soon, when a coming event will dispel all our hard feelings by the promises it will bring.

Marie GRANT-TANERAN

Upon receiving the letter, George Durieux went up to L'Oustaou. There was a chilly fog that morning. He came back slowly at noontime and returned just as slowly after lunch. One by one, he meticulously filled the waiting hours.

He ended up on the station platform well before the train's arrival. Maud appeared warmly dressed already, as they were in Paris, her features somewhat drawn, with a wide-eyed, anxious look. She waited until George came to her, his eyes fixed on hers.

Her gloved hand was in George's, both of them inert. But all at once, her staunch look gave way and her hand regained its strength and expressiveness. "Do you have a car? It's for the suitcase . . ." She had a big, brand-new suitcase of the kind used by boarders: her mother's final act of generosity. They had wanted to do things decently . . .

They left. In the distance, alongside the highway, Uderan lifted up its treetops in the moonlight. "You know that they had seriously committed themselves to a deal?" said Maud, making an effort to address George in a familiar way. "Mother even received the fifty thousand francs. Did you know? What a laugh, all the same!"

Her cheerfulness grated in the cold wind. She snuggled up against him. The car was open, and the wind was howling over their heads. "You'll see how windy it is at Bordeaux on certain days!" said George.

"At Bordeaux?" Maud asked gently.

"Yes," he answered, "and as for the fifty thousand francs, don't worry, they're already taken care of."

There was a long silence as she grew accustomed to the idea. "They'll be awfully happy in Paris. You did that to please them?"

"Yes," replied George, "why not please them?"

❖

TRANSLATOR'S
AFTERWORD

KELSEY L. HASKETT

A study of the place of *The Impudent Ones* (*Les impudents*) in relation to the totality of Duras's work, with respect to both narrative style and content, reveals two prominent threads woven throughout the novel: the introduction of a complicated web of family relations that will dominate the entire fabric of Duras's later work, and the impressive use of descriptive passages—a salient feature that carries over into much of the author's future writing.

The stylistic differences between this novel, in which Duras deploys her skills as a novelist for the first time, and future novels, have long been acknowledged. Compared to later novels, known for their style *dépouillé*, in which everything is pared down to the essentials, the use of a more traditional narrative style in *The Impudent Ones* is evident. Yet even in this debut work, lacking the characteristics of her later inimitable style, Duras's ability as a writer is irrefutable. Descriptions of specific time and place ring out with great authenticity, while the attention given to the depiction of characters also discloses her keen powers of observation. The extensive development of detail that typifies this beginning novel is perhaps to be expected, given the close relationship between the author and her subject matter, in terms of the setting, the composition of the main family, reflective of her own, and certain people and events that helped inspire her novel, although recast in a new light to form a convincing story that emerges from her imagination. Duras's fiction generally stems from deeply embedded memories of the past, assimilated and transformed by her psyche, as she crafts them into a novel that becomes a world in itself, a blend of personal experience and creative transformation. By drawing from the start on the resources of her intuitive inner self, as shown in this novel, Duras succeeds in bringing to life a region and a people that strongly impacted her early years, while at the same time insightfully portraying the first of a long line of female characters who are not strictly autobiographical, in the usual sense of the word, but are nevertheless based on her own person.

The principal significance of this first novel, from the standpoint of its content, derives from its relationship to the entirety of Duras's writings. Not only does *The Impudent Ones* lay the groundwork for her later "autobiographical fiction," as it is called, but countless words, phrases, situations, and character types are reproduced throughout Duras's work, contributing to the obsessive themes that define her as an author. Most important, the family relationships developed here reflect those that she unremittingly shapes and reshapes in succeeding works: the domineering mother who fosters a codependent relationship with her older son to the detriment of her other children, especially her daughter; the cruel, unscrupulous older brother who contributes to his own demise and that of his family; the younger brother, inoffensive, but generally up to no good (especially in the first novel); and the daughter, who suffers from rejection and hostility while seeking love and acceptance in fleeing from her family.

Those who are familiar with Duras's works will find here the first portrayals of the key family characters, conflicts, and ensuing narratives, in their various iterations, whether in the semi-autobiographical works or inserted less conspicuously in Duras's fiction. For readers new to her writing, this novel could well be viewed as an invitation to pursue a world-class author whose variations on a central theme focus on questions of family life, rejection, the search for identity, and the quest for an elusive love meant to overcome the dejection of the past and the tragedy of life's ongoing void, especially for Duras's female protagonists.

Both textual fragments and narrative details in this initial novel evoke multiple later works. For example, in her second novel, Duras reworks the story developed in *The Impudent Ones* of a dysfunctional family that "lives in disorder"—the word "disorder" appearing frequently in later novels—while the mother dreams of living a "quiet life," the title of Duras's second novel: *La vie tranquille*. The deep concern shared by the mother and daughter in *The Impudent Ones*, when the brothers don't come home at night, is amplified in the third novel, *The Sea Wall*, where parallel relationships exist between the mother, the favored son, and the daughter. Despite their mutual grievances and their desire to separate in all the works portraying the family, a strong sense of solidarity binds the family members together, right from the very first novel.

The older brother's brutal ascendancy over the family, first portrayed in *The Impudent Ones*, becomes a constant factor in later novels, in which the sister's identification with him is nevertheless as powerful as her hatred of this abusive sibling. Her desire to see him dead in both *The Impudent Ones* and *The Lover* is played out in substitutionary form in *La vie tranquille*, which opens with the younger brother killing the uncle, who has also brought shame and ruin upon his family. The daughter's perceived rejection by her mother because of an illegitimate pregnancy at the end of *The Impudent Ones* is hinted at elsewhere, but blows up into a catastrophic relationship in *The Vice-Consul*, where the pregnant daughter, expelled from her home, is forced into a life of begging and prostitution through her mother's cruel rejection. Not only has this element of the story persisted in the author's imagination, but it has intensified—through emotions that have obviously deepened with time. The absence of the father during the family's entire stay at their domain of Uderan in *The Impudent Ones* is reinforced by his minimal role in the second novel and complete elimination in other novels, corresponding to the early passing of Duras's own father, before her childhood stay at Platier, the family domain.

One of the most striking similarities in terms of character portrayal occurs in the person of Jacques, who reappears as the protagonist in *Whole Days in the Trees* (a short story, play, and film). The mirror image of Jacques in the first novel, the second Jacques has all the moral failings of the first, and an identical relationship with his mother (the same that appears in the other novels focused on the family). An inveterate gambler who is not above stealing from his mother in *Whole Days in the Trees*, he also demoralizes his family in *The Impudent Ones* through his reckless spending and continual need to beg for money from the rest of the family. In both stories he is unwilling to work, spends his time in a bar and dance hall, and insists on being in control of the people and events around him, even though he has no control over his own life. Despite his hardened character, he is the preferred child of his mother, who is ready to sacrifice her life and her other family ties to maintain an exclusive relationship with this son incapable of taking on the responsibilities of adult life. And yet, she occasionally questions her abnormally prolonged maternal role and muses in *The Impudent Ones* that "one should be careful of children who plunder everything one has"—words that could easily have been spoken by the mother of Jacques in *Whole Days in the Trees*.

This older brother shows up much later, of course, in *The Lover*, followed by *The North China Lover*, where his continued pillaging of the family is accompanied by a lurking threat of violence that kindles an even greater fear in his sister than that which appears in the first novel. It is not so much his gambling as his opium addiction that proves to be the underlying cause of his behavior in these later novels. Although fictionalized in many aspects, these semi-autobiographical novels relate nonetheless impactful emotions consciously or unconsciously registered by the author while encountering familial and other situations in life, which gradually evolve into story form. Duras herself claimed to have lived her life as a novel, and when queried about her life, she replied that her life was in her books—a statement implying both her intimate inner self and her more visible outer life.

Thus, when Maud fears her elder brother's meanness and authority in *The Impudent Ones*, when the sister dreads the complicity of her brother with her mother who beats her in *The Sea Wall*, and when the narrator depicts the violence of the older brother in *The Lover*, who inflicts his reign of terror on both her and her younger brother, Duras seems to be transmitting a transformed, composite portrait of her life with her siblings, not necessarily as revealed in actual events, but as filtered through her subconscious. Duras's second brother in *The Impudent Ones* corresponds to the one looked upon almost as her child in *La vie tranquille* (where the narrator holds a secret, passionate love for him), and to the adored "younger brother," with whom the narrator has a similar relationship in the later semi-autobiographical novels.

Even more significant than the figure of the two brothers is the mother figure, who dominates the life of the female protagonist in all the novels in which the mother–daughter relationship is depicted. In *The Impudent Ones*, where this relationship first plays out, the strained relationship between the mother and daughter results from both the mother's disproportionate love for the older brother and the daughter's fear that her mother will learn of her relationship with George, which transgresses the family's moral code (at least, for the daughter). These concerns carry over into each of the novels set in French Indochina, in which the mother's treatment of the daughter becomes increasingly violent. In *The Sea Wall*, Suzanne is physically, verbally, and psychologically abused by the mother, who yells at her, accuses her of immorality, and beats her mercilessly at times, with the complicity of the brother. Using as a pretext that Suzanne has slept with the son of a wealthy Chinese businessman to obtain from him an enormous diamond (which, in fact, the mother has stolen from Suzanne), the mother takes out all her frustrations in life on her daughter, who becomes a scapegoat for her enormous failures. In *The Lover*, the daughter is also beaten and slapped around by her mother, who again is encouraged to do so by her older brother, and in *The North China Lover* this kind of treatment is mentioned in the dialogue.

In each of these novels an extreme tension develops between the daughter and the mother, even turning into a love-hate relationship in *The Lover*, but always caused by a deep sense of rejection on the part of the daughter, including Maud, at the end of *The Impudent Ones*, when she becomes pregnant with George's child. The less violent relationship in this first novel returns to some degree in *The North China Lover*, where in a more fanciful way the author introduces surprising dialogues between the lover and the mother, whereby the mutual acceptance of the two seems to introduce a hidden desire for reconciliation on the part of Duras in relation to these two central figures portrayed in her works. Nevertheless, the plight of the daughter in each of the novels is much less than enviable when it comes to the mother–daughter relationship (as well as the relationship with the brothers) and produces an extreme and often overwhelming sadness in the daughter's life.

Other parallels with future novels extend beyond family relationships. The figure of an unreported drowning victim appears in the first two works, with Maud, in the first novel, failing to mention the drowned woman she spots in the river, with serious consequences for the plot, and Francine, the main character in *La vie tranquille*, leaving undisclosed the fate of a man who drowns in the sea before her very eyes. At the end of *The Lover*, a young man also throws himself from an ocean liner into the sea, as the narrator and her family cross the ocean—seemingly unrelated events, but producing unsettling echoes.

Certain details of the relationship between Maud and George in *The Impudent Ones* are reflective of the relationship of the couple in *The Lover*, without the two sets of lovers being necessarily identical. In both cases, the young woman shows a sudden disinterest in her lover upon arriving at his place with the intent of giving herself to him for the first time, her interest being curiously deflected to her surroundings. However, it is only in the first novel that she is briefly seized with a keen sense of modesty and self-defense that she forces herself to overcome. Following that, the frustration of a relationship with no apparent future and seemingly devoid of love characterizes both of the couples.

When Maud's first encounter with George is discovered by her family and their host family in the region, who are also upset by her scandalous absence during an entire day, her shame is intensified as the others "devour her pitilessly with their gaze" while she tries to eat her evening meal, suggestive of Anne Desbaresdes's silent ordeal during the lavish reception in *Moderato cantabile*. When Maud is with George for what he thinks is the last time prior to her leaving, he kisses her, but "almost without desire," because of her lack of commitment. "Their joined lips were cold, but they preferred this contact to that of their eyes, which fled from each other." This, too, reflects the lifeless parting moments of Anne and

Chauvin in their last encounter in *Moderato cantabile*. The final reconciliation between Maud and George, however, appears to be unique to this beginning work, where love brings about the kind of resolution that will rarely, if ever, be reproduced in later works.

Turning now to questions of style, the descriptive qualities of *The Impudent Ones* are principally linked to place. Situated in the southwest of France, near the town from which the author drew her pseudonym, *The Impudent Ones* reveals the profound attachment of Duras to the land. Images of hills, valleys, rivers, woods, and fields captivate the reader through their beauty and accuracy in relation to the region where Duras spent relatively brief but memorable periods of her childhood and youth.

Nature is not merely portrayed in general terms, but the precise names of birds, trees, and various types of vegetation create a strong sense of local color that draws the reader into the richness of the landscape and the atmosphere of the passing seasons of this region Duras loved: "Because of the recent rains, the grass was thick and luscious, and the air gave off the fragrance of sap. Thrushes flew low over the fields and the velvety whir of their wings made a rustling noise. From the tops of the tall poplar trees of the Riotor, goldfinches were singing, infusing the azure sky with their voluptuous, triumphant notes." Richly figurative descriptions of evolving moments of the day and night also contribute to a lyrical effect, as do the multiple depictions of weather—unbearable heat, pounding rain, limpid skies—while all the senses are engaged in the production of a very natural and convincing backdrop to the story.

Although Duras does not appear to return to the same

kind of elaborate background description in her later works, her sensitivity to nature and to transitions in time that affect human experience continues to undergird her writing. In *Moderato cantabile*, for example, the glorious arrival of evening, with all its resplendent colors, contrasts with the suffocating atmosphere of the piano lesson in the first chapter. Nature, the embodiment of freedom, stands in opposition to the sense of imprisonment created by inner spaces and the impositions of society. While the young pupil, dominated by his teacher, can only glimpse the wondrous transformation of the evening sky outside, other children, unimpeded, stand motionless on the quay, awed by the breathtaking hues of the sunset. In *The Impudent Ones*, Maud is just as moved by evening's approach, even though it fills her with very divided emotions. "Maud wondered what this gentleness that arose with the evening was, so hard on her heart."

Despite the rift between nature's perfection and her unhappy inner state, she is nevertheless attracted to the natural environment, to the point of leaving the door of the family estate open to the nocturnal sounds, scents, and breezes that invade her bedroom at night and unite her with the outdoors: "Maud fell asleep as soon as the breeze died down of itself in the forest . . . but she woke up abruptly as soon as a fresh breath of wind carrying all the surrounding fragrances returned. . . It had swept the great depths of the valley, carrying with it, as a result, the scent of bitter algae and decayed leaves."

The ability of nature to penetrate the characters' lives is also evidenced in *The Lover*, where the young girl crossing the Mekong, symbol of the change she is about to undergo, is strangely sensitive to the hazy light over the water and the river's blurry shores, even as she feels the current flowing noiselessly beneath her like the blood in her veins. Whether revealed in the light of dawn or the dark blue of night, the use of description drawn from nature to create a compelling ambiance and enhance the meaning of the text has always enriched Duras's writing, from her first novel onward.

Other points of comparison, both major and minor, are easily discernable for readers familiar with Duras. For example, it is George, Maud's lover, who pays the debt owed by the family at the end of the first novel, and the Chinese lover who pays the family's debt at the end of *The North China Lover*. The interplay between various works obviously provides much scope for reflection and analysis. Like a sapling sending out its shoots in multiple directions, the words, characters, and essential components of this initial novel continue to expand and produce an abundance of interrelated themes, as the literary production of the author advances.

In every case, the creative elements related to Duras's life, and the way in which she interprets and reframes them, contribute to the extraordinary unity of all of her work, including novel, theater, and film. *The Vice-Consul*, later filmed as *India Song*, exemplifies how characters from earlier works may later take on new and sometimes bolder characterizations, such as the beggar-woman's harsh, unfeeling mother and the enigmatic vice-consul, whose violent, anti-social behavior in both the novel and film evoke that of the older brother depicted in Duras's works from the beginning. Hence, it would be difficult to overestimate the role of *The Impudent Ones* in paving the way for a fuller elucidation of the entire corpus of Duras's work.

A further factor shedding light on the subject of Duras's narrative style is the reception of the novel at the time of its publication. Submitted as *La famille Taneran* in 1941 to the large French publisher Gallimard, it was read and appreciated by the highly esteemed Raymond Queneau, even though the publisher turned it down, citing mainly a lack of cohesiveness in the writing style and plot. In 1943, despite noting similar weaknesses, the publisher Plon decided to bring out the novel as *Les impudents*. Not only was the title changed, but it was at this point that Marguerite adopted the pseudonym Duras, taken both from the novel's setting and from the region most connected in her mind to her father, and becoming her name for all posterity.

Although the novel did not create much of a stir when it was published, it was well-received by critic Ramon Fernandez, who discusses it very positively in the newspaper *Panorama,* in May 1943, at the time of the novel's publication. He lauds the author for her skillful handling of the characters, her excellent mastery of their psychology, and the creation of an intense and tragic atmosphere. He finds that the main character's inner thoughts express a rare candor, while her feelings and actions seem both strange and natural. The novel abounds, he claims, in astute impressions of both the landscape and the human soul, to which the reader may have been oblivious, but can relate at the same time. Fernandez concludes that once the author has honed her writing style, which sometimes wavers, she will have perfected her unquestionable talent.

As Duras gained greater recognition for her following works, she herself became aware of the shortcomings of her first novel and began to omit it when referencing her work, resulting in the novel's disappearance from the bibliographies of her works for quite some time. As her style evolved, however, and she became more affirmed as an author, eventually gaining acclaim as the award-winning author of *The Lover*, readers began to take an increased interest in Duras's first novel, long neglected, and it was republished by Gallimard in 1992.

The problems of lucidity and cohesiveness, first recognized by the two French presses that dealt with the novel, still present a challenge to the reader and the translator today, not only in regard to the plot, which at times lacks clarity, but also in relation to the interplay between characters. Unclear antecedents for pronouns and oblique grammatical constructions are among the stylistic challenges that often make it difficult to determine precisely who is speaking or the intended meaning of a given phrase or sentence. To overcome these ambiguities and facilitate a greater enjoyment of the text, the goal of the present translation has been to render the reading of the novel as intelligible as possible for the reader. This has been accomplished through the addition of occasional words and phrases, not in the original, to provide smoother transitions as the text unfolds, and by the replacement of pronouns by proper nouns in dialogues and interactions that are less than clear. In every case, adherence to the original meaning of the text has been of utmost concern.

In recent years, *The Impudent Ones* has taken on new meaning for readers and scholars around the world, as it has come to be appreciated not only for its significance to the rest of Duras's work, but increasingly for its intrinsic value as a novel. Although already translated into a number of other languages, this first translation of the novel into English, some seventy-eight years after its original publication, will now allow the novel to be accessed by a much broader readership. In doing so, it will reveal to a new public the starting point of the exceptional qualities of observation and description that characterize Duras's celebrated later works, while affording a view of the renowned author as she first gains a foothold in the world of writing. Of no less consequence, *The Impudent Ones* also provides a record of a time, place, and personal connection that were undeniably of great significance to Marguerite Duras, not only as she began her career, but throughout her life.

THE STORY BEHIND
THE IMPUDENT ONES

JEAN VALLIER

In February 1941, Gaston Gallimard, the founder and owner of the famed French publishing house that bore his name, received a manuscript in the mail, accompanied by the following letter:

Monsieur,

My name is perhaps not totally unknown to you, because I co-authored the book The French Empire, *published by your house last year. But the manuscript I am submitting to you today—La* famille Taneran—*has no connection to this first book, which was for me but a work for hire. I now wish to make my debut as a novelist. The manuscript I am sending you was read by Messrs. Henri Clouard, André Thérive and Pierre Lafue, who liked it very much and strongly encouraged me to have it published. I trust their opinion. I hope that it will correspond to yours. I should be glad in any case to receive your answer without too much delay.*

Yours faithfully, Marguerite Donnadieu[1]

_____

1 Gallimard archives.

This letter, addressed to the publisher of literary giants such as Proust, Gide, and Paul Valéry, was not written by a timorous would-be novelist. Apart from the fact that her name had appeared the year before on the cover of *L'empire français*, she had reason to believe that the names of the three gentlemen who vouched for the quality of her manuscript would not fail to impress her correspondent: Henri Clouard and André Thérive were at the time two of France's most influential literary critics, and Pierre Lafue, a novelist and a respected critic himself, was a governmental agent who had played a part in the publication of her first book and was now one of her most devoted friends. She knew he had privileged access to Gaston Gallimard.

Contrary to the legend of poverty and abuse still hanging over the story of her early life, when the future Marguerite Duras wrote her first novel—thanks in great part to the college education her mother enabled her to receive—the young writer had grown into a secure, self-assured young woman.[2] Now twenty-six and married, she had joined the Parisian bourgeoisie and was not easily daunted—a side of her nature she would continue to display for the rest of her life.

Born near Saigon in 1914, Marguerite Donnadieu was the daughter of two teachers who worked in the educational system put in place by the French in Indochina, a colony com-

---

2 The legend that Marguerite Duras created herself—that she grew up extremely poor and suffered at the hands of a dominating and indifferent mother and an abusive older brother—rests mostly on two of her books, *The Sea Wall* and *Wartime Writings*. Inspired by real-life family events, these are nevertheless mostly fictional accounts. Duras's *Wartime Writings*, which include ostensible reminiscences about her youth, are not actual diaries and need to be analyzed carefully in order to separate fact from fiction.

prised of what is now Vietnam, as well as Cambodia and Laos. Her father, Henri Donnadieu, born in southwestern France in 1872, held a university degree in natural sciences, which he taught occasionally in Saigon and Hanoi between assignments as a school director and education supervisor. Her mother, born Marie Legrand in the Pas-de-Calais in 1877, trained at a teacher's college in Lille before going to Indochina in 1905, where she taught and was ultimately placed in charge of several establishments for Vietnamese girls. When they met, Henri had two sons from a previous marriage who returned to France after their mother died. He married Marie Legrand in Saigon in 1908 and had two sons with her before Marguerite's birth: Pierre, her *frère aîné*, in 1910, and Paul, her *petit frère*, in 1911.

The three children traveled to France several times, first with both parents during World War I when Marguerite was still a toddler, then with their widowed mother, following the premature death of their father to malaria in December 1921. The family remained in France between 1922 and 1924. They lived in a small village in the Lot-et-Garonne, east of Bordeaux, in a house Henri Donnadieu had bought near the place of his birth, presumably for his retirement. Marie Donnadieu having decided to return to Indochina to resume her career, they left for Saigon in the summer of 1924. After seven years in the Mekong Delta where their mother had been posted, in 1931, Marguerite and her brother Paul returned with her to France for one year (Pierre, the eldest, had been sent back to France in 1924 to study). They lived on the outskirts of Paris, where Marguerite attended a private school in the sixteenth arrondissement and passed the first part of her *baccalauréat*. Back in Saigon, she completed her secondary studies at the city's lycée in 1933. In the fall, she left Indochina for the last time, returning to Paris to further her education. She attended law school at the Sorbonne for four years, graduating in 1937 with a degree in common law and political economics. In June of that year, she was hired by the French Ministry of the Colonies to write promotional materials. At twenty-three, she was now independent financially and free to live as she pleased. She was making a good salary, could afford nice clothes, and drove her own Ford coupé convertible, which she used to explore the countryside or go to the seashore with her beau of the moment.

L'empire français

Georges Mandel, a major figure in the history of the Third Republic, was appointed Minister of the Colonies in 1938, and brought with him Pierre Lafue, his speechwriter. Mandel was determined to use his position to counter Germany's war propaganda, issuing a continuous stream of interventions in the press, on the state-controlled radio network, and in weekly newsreels shown in movie theaters. In 1939, in order to publicize the part that French overseas possessions could play in the looming conflict in terms of foot soldiers and war materiel, he asked his staff to put together a book about the country's colonial empire. His press attaché, a young man named Philippe Roques, took up that task with the help of the Indochina-born Mademoiselle Donnadieu, whose own pen had caught the attention of her superiors. Her name ultimately appeared on the book's cover, next to the name of her colleague. Gallimard agreed to publish the book based on an advance order from the ministry for three thousand copies, to be given out at the Salon de la France d'Outremer planned to be held in Paris the following year.

That September, the Nazis invaded Poland. Despite the war, the "Overseas France" salon opened on schedule on May 6, 1940, with Albert Lebrun, the president of the French Republic, and Georges Mandel, the Minister of the Colonies, in attendance. At the salon's entrance, fresh off the printing press, *L'empire français* was offered to visitors. The co-authors would not enjoy their nascent notoriety for long, however. Four days later, Hitler's armies, bypassing the "unassailable" Maginot Line in the East, invaded France from Belgium. Within weeks, as German tanks continued their progression from the north, Paris was declared an open city to avoid its destruction. All the French ministries had to leave town.

Marguerite Duras left the French capital with Lafue and Roques on June 9, first for the Loire Valley, where the ministries took temporary refuge, then for Bordeaux five days later, where the French government withdrew as the soldiers of the Third Reich marched down the Champs-Élysées. At the end of the month, after fighting had stopped (the armistice was signed on June 22), she left Bordeaux with Lafue and went with him to Brive-la-Gaillarde, a small city near the Dordogne where Lafue's brother and his family lived. After a few weeks in Brive, she returned to Paris in mid-August. (Philippe Roques joined the Résistance movement and went on to serve as a secret agent between de Gaulle and Mandel, as well as between Churchill and Mandel, until he was captured and killed by the Gestapo in 1943.)

A Married Woman Under Vichy

Much had changed since she left the French capital. A new government had been born from the defeat of the French army, with la République française ceding control to the authoritarian l'État français, led by Marshal Philippe Pétain, a hero of World War I who was recalled from his ambassadorial post in Madrid. Not given to progressive thoughts, the eighty-year-old Pétain, under the pretext of sparing the French further miseries, was soon advocating cooperation with the invaders and taking a series of repressive measures in order to rid France of its "past errors." "Liberté, égalité, fraternité" was now replaced by "Travail, famille, patrie (Work, family, fatherland)," a motto more in tune with the return to ancestral values preached by the old marshal and his entourage. From now on women were expected to stay home. Unless they were under permanent contract with the state (such as teachers in public schools), married women would no longer be authorized to work in the French administration.

Marguerite Duras's position as an auxiliary with the Ministry of the Colonies was about to be terminated. Newly unemployed, she would have to depend on her husband's salary, a situation that circumstances related to the war had made problematic. In September 1939, a few weeks after the hostilities started, she had married Robert Antelme, the son of a tax officer in the affluent sixth arrondissement of Paris whom she had met at the Sorbonne in 1937. Three years her junior, he was called for military duty in 1938, shortly after graduating from law school, and sent directly to the front the following year. When he returned to civilian life in the summer of 1940, Robert Antelme had never been employed and now had to look for a job. Through the intervention of François Piétri, a first cousin of his mother who headed several ministries before the war and was now part of Vichy's first government, he was hired by the Paris Préfecture de Police as a temporary assistant in the prefect's office. (He would join the Ministry of Industry eight month later, before being reassigned to the Ministry of the Interior). François Piétri could have perhaps intervene at the Ministry of the Colonies on behalf of his young cousin's wife, but at the end of that summer, as the government was reshuffled he was let go and sent to Madrid to succeed Marshal Pétain as ambassador to Franco's Spain, a position he held until 1944.

We do not know if Marguerite Duras was distraught at having lost her job, and with it her financial independence, or if she was happy to be able to devote herself fully to writing, thus realizing her early ambition (at the age of twelve, she had allegedly confided to her mother that she wanted to be a writer). What we do know, thanks to a membership card from the library of the University of Paris dated August 20, 1940, signed Marguerite Antelme, is that she was authorized to work in the reading room of the Bibliothèque Sainte-Geneviève from that date until the end of November. This is when she wrote La famille Taneran, later to be renamed Les impudents, published now in English for the first time as The Impudent Ones. She may have started a first draft during her stay in Brive-la-Gaillarde, where she could discuss her work with her friend Pierre Lafue, but the bulk of the novel must have been written during the first fall and early winter of the German occupation.

The Taneran Family

This family is composed of the father and the mother (already advanced in age), of two sons and one daughter. The eldest of the brothers, Jacques is a mawkish lout, cowardly and spiteful; the younger one remains uncommunicative; Maud, the daughter, romantic, passionate, vindictive, who feels unloved or forsaken, in any case misunderstood, goes to live for a few weeks with a man she has met. Her mother comes to fetch her, does not upbraid her too much. The mother cares above all for her elder son, and, perhaps because Maud is fallen and no longer superior to Jacques, she does not blame Maud for this transgression. Maud, intending to show herself worthy of the baseness one attributes to her, denounces her brother to the police for a scam of fake bills of exchange.[3]

Such was the less-than-glowing reader's report on the manuscript for Gallimard, written by Marcel Arland, a distinguished writer and winner of the Prix Goncourt in 1929 for *L'Ordre*, a novel about another dysfunctional family in provincial France between the two wars.

Like so many first novels, *The Impudent Ones* is partly autobiographical. The portrait of the divided Taneran family found in this book also foreshadows the one the author would paint later in works such as *Whole Days in the Trees* and *The Lover*. Freely mixing fiction and reality, the family

---

3 Gallimard archives.

portrait is drawn here through the subjective memory of an aspiring writer trying to come to terms with an emotionally charged adolescence.[4] To write her novel, Marguerite Duras drew direct inspiration from events that had affected her and her family during the year they spent in France in 1931–32, and many details suggest that the story takes place in the early 1930s.

The main characters seem to have been modeled on the author herself, as well as on her immediate relatives. Under the English-sounding name of Maud Grant, the anguished heroine at the center of the story brings to mind a young Marguerite Donnadieu, only taller and more self-assured than she was at the time. In the same way, Mrs. Grant-Taneran was fashioned after her own mother, like her a widow with the first name Marie, and also advanced in age (Mrs. Donnadieu was then fifty-four, going on fifty-five).

Jacques, the dissolute troublemaker, is easily identified as a version of Pierre Donnadieu, Marguerite's "hated" older brother. Although only four year her senior, he is made to be more contemptible in the novel by being past forty and still without any occupation or sense of purpose (Maud decries her brother's "shameless desire . . . to live the way he wanted to"). The author's late father was brought back to life under the insipid figure of Mr. Taneran, Mrs. Grant's second husband, a civil servant who "at one time . . . had had a respectable

---

4 In a copy of her book that she gave to her companion Dionys Mascolo in 1943, Marguerite Duras wrote: "This book fell from me: the dread and the desire born from the hard part of a childhood no doubt not easy."

career teaching natural sciences at the high school in Auch," where he met his wife. Henri, the son they had together, can be viewed as a substitute for Paul Donnadieu, the author's second brother, or as a salute to Jacques Donnadieu, one of her half brothers, to whom the novel is dedicated.[5]

The settings of *Les impudents*, a residential suburb of the French capital and a village in the southwestern part of the country, are versions, under altered names, of places where the author lived when she came back to France as a child and then again for a few weeks as an adolescent in 1931. In the opening chapter, the apartment occupied by the Grant-Taneran family, the *septième* from which Maud contemplates a landscape extending to "the somber streak of the hills of Sèvres," appears to be the very same seventh-floor apartment her mother rented in 1931 in a new art-deco building still standing today in its gleaming whiteness at 16, avenue Victor-Hugo, in Vanves, west of Paris. In the novel, walking through the streets of Clamart (Vanves), she can see from a distance "the huge white hulk of the building in which they lived." Taking us on a tour of the apartment, the narrator takes care to point out the Henri II sideboard in their dining room (for many French readers, a sure sign of petit-bourgeois taste), lest we think of the family as fashion-minded sophisticates.

---

5 Jean and Jacques Donnadieu, born respectively in 1899 and 1904, were the two sons Marguerite Duras's father had from his first marriage. Although she knew Jean Donnadieu well at the time she wrote *Les impudents*, she would never meet his brother again after she returned to Indochina during World War I as a three-year-old child.

A Bourgeois Drama

Mrs. Grant-Taneran may be a petit-bourgeois who cooks her own meals (by contrast, in 1931, Mrs. Donnadieu brought her cook with her to Paris from Indochina), but the mother in *The Impudent Ones* owns land in the southwest, an estate she presumably acquired with the savings of her first husband, a tax collector (like the author's father-in-law). With some major changes in the chronology and the nature of the auto-biographical events that inspired it, the story unfolds around that prized Uderan estate, "located in the southwest Lot, in the rough and unpopulated part of Upper Quercy, on the edge of Dordogne and Lot-et-Garonne."

With some minor geographical realignments, one can easily make the short trip on a map to the estate Marguerite Duras's father bought a few weeks before he died unexpectedly in France in 1921, at age forty-nine, during a medical leave of absence. This is the rural environment where, between the ages of eight and ten, his daughter spent two years with her mother and her two brothers, and which the author would evoke in vivid detail in *The Impudent Ones*. *Le domaine de Platier* (its real name) originally comprised forty-five acres of woods, vineyards, orchards, meadows, and a tobacco plantation, situated near the small village of Pardaillan (The Pardal in the novel), a few kilometers east of the historical hill-town of Duras (Ostel in the novel)—the town from which Marguerite later took her nom de plume.

When Marguerite Duras returned to France with her mother and her brother Paul in the spring of 1931 (Pierre was by then living in Paris), the *maison de maître* in which they had previously lived had been emptied of its furniture and unoccupied for several years.[6] As it was now unhabitable, they had to take board and lodgings with neighbors for a few weeks while Marie Donnadieu organized the sale of the estate, which included an old farmhouse in the back of the main dwelling that housed a sharecropping couple and their daughter, still tending the land for the absentee owner.

These characters are all made to play a part in *The Impudent Ones*—the neighbors as the Pecresse family, the tenant farmers as the Dedde family. The Pecresses would not mind marrying their son to their guest's daughter (thus acquiring a stake in the estate), but they are kept firmly in their assigned rank on the social ladder. The narrator takes pains to explain: "Even if the Grant-Tanerans were only bourgeois folk without distinction, Uderan, their land, conferred on them a kind of nobility." Thus, while Maud is addressed as *Mademoiselle Grant*, or "*la Demoiselle*" and her mother as *Madame*, or *Madame Grant-Taneran*, the neighbors by contrast are referred to by the less respectful *La Pécresse, la mère Pécresse, Le Père Pécresse, le jeune Pécresse;* and the tenant farmers as *La Dedde, le père Dedde, la fille Dedde*—the way people in the countryside called each other at the time.

Many of the inhabitants of Pardaillan figure in the novel as extras, vividly rendered through the author's observant eye and ear for popular parlance ("in the thick dialect of the

---

6 Henri Donnadieu died without leaving a will. The Platier estate became embroiled in a lengthy legal action initiated by his brother, intent on ensuring the rights of Marguerite Duras's half brothers. In 1924, before going back to Indochina, Marie Donnadieu was able to buy back the property, but the main house had to be emptied of all its contents, which were sold at public auction. When they came back in 1931, the house had been sealed off for several years.

Dordogne"). Lording over the locals, Mrs. Grant-Taneran gives a *grand dîner* for the villagers in her dilapidated mansion. The guests are seated according to rank, and what ensues is a small comedy of manners in the spirit of Gustave Flaubert or Guy de Maupassant.

In another parallel to the author's life, the reader is informed at the beginning of the story that "Jacques had just lost his wife . . . She had died that very day following a car accident." In real life, before his mother and siblings arrived in France in 1931, Pierre Donnadieu, then nearing twenty-one, had been living in Paris with a wealthy woman who died in a car accident—a possible suicide.

The lover that Maud takes up when the family relocates to their summer estate appears to be modeled on Jean Lagrolet, the handsome scion of an upper-middle-class family, whom Marguerite Duras met at the Sorbonne and dated for two years in the 1930s. The public scandal at the heart of the novel, loss of prestige for Maud's family, and secret pregnancy that ultimately shatters the clan also seem to have been inspired by real-life events. In 1932, at the age of eighteen, Marguerite Duras was dating one of her schoolmates from the private establishment she was attending—the son of a prominent family of lawyers—and became pregnant. Contrary to the loveless but conventional ending in the novel, however, no wedding was celebrated. A discreet abortion was arranged, which the author would reveal much later in her career.[7]

---

7 In 1971, Marguerite Duras joined a group of prominent women who signed a petition calling for the French law criminalizing abortion to be repealed. Simone de Beauvoir (who wrote the petition), Françoise Sagan, Catherine Deneuve, and Ariane Mnouchkine were among the one hundred and twenty-three women who revealed publicly that they had had an abortion.

Literary Influences

In his assessment of the novel for Gallimard, Marcel Arland wrote: "It is very awkward, rather badly put together, confused . . . rudimentary, sometimes incoherent—but there is here a rather strange atmosphere (à la Mauriac and *Wuthering Heights*), a certain grasp of family turmoil, of cruelty, of moral degradation."[8]

That Marguerite Duras was influenced by François Mauriac there is little doubt. She was an avid reader, fully cognizant of the prevailing trends in French fiction between the two wars. While studying law at the Sorbonne, she audited public classes on contemporary literature given by Fortunat Strowski, an eminent specialist who coincidentally had been Mauriac's teacher at the University of Bordeaux before World War I. At the time she was writing *The Impudent Ones*, Mauriac had become one of the most eminent French novelists (he was elected to the prestigious Académie française in 1933). His stories of divided and secretive provincial families from the *grande bourgeoisie*, such as *Thérèse Desqueyroux*, published in 1927, and *Le noeud de vipères*, published in 1932, inspired legions of aspiring writers at odds with their bourgeois environment. Mauriac himself was an admirer of Paul Bourget, the late nineteenth-century author of celebrated *romans psychologiques* set in upper-middle-class families, including a series of novels purporting to analyze "women's emotions." (Bourget was supposedly Henry James's favorite French writer.)

In the late 1930s, the future Marguerite Duras was a regu-

---

8 Gallimard archives.

lar at the Mathurins, the Paris theater directed by Georges and Ludmilla Pitoëff, where she saw Ibsen's *A Doll's House* and Chekhov's *The Seagull*. In her novel, Maud is a romantic young woman: "If he [Durieux] loved her, one day he would devote all his moments, his leisure time, to her." The man she compromises herself with happens to be a gentleman who tells her, "I think it would be more fitting on my part to speak to your mother." Maud may have loved him at the beginning of their affair, but, like Nora in *A Doll's House* or Thérèse Desqueyroux, she ends up locked in a loveless marriage, victim of the social conventions of her milieu. Like Mauriac's *grands bourgeois*, her mother puts respectability above everything else. A *fille-mère* would be an indelible stain on the Grant-Tanerans' standing in society. It is also worth noting that, as in Mauriac's *Viper's Tangle*, money plays a significant part in *The Impudent Ones*. Financial needs motivate most of Jacques's intrigues. Mrs. Grant-Taneran herself displays miserly habits and uses money to keep her favorite son under her power.

The influence of *Wuthering Heights*, underlined in Marcel Arland's evaluation of the manuscript, must have seemed self-evident at the time. Emily Brontë's classic of Victorian literature was popular with French readers—all the more after the release of William Wyler's movie in Paris in 1939. No less than three new French translations of the novel were published between 1925 and 1937. As an ardent anglophile, Marguerite Duras was familiar with the works of the Brontë Sisters. *Les hauts de Hurlevent*—the French title most often used—was one of her favorite books. The rivalries between the protagonists, as well as the landscape surrounding their coveted estate—"the rough and unpopulated part of Upper Quercy" in *The Impudent Ones*; the Yorkshire Moors in *Wuthering Heights*—invite comparison between the two novels. One can find other similarities: like Catherine Earnshaw, Maud Grant is impulsive and independent. Like her, Maud reconciles herself to marrying a wealthy man she does not love, and like "Cathy," Maud is the character who keeps the story moving to its conclusion. It is doubtful, however, that Marguerite Duras drew more than remote inspiration from *Wuthering Heights*. If Jacques Grant shares some of Heathcliff's innate cruelty, he does not have the dark, romantic stature of Brontë's hero. The result of Jacques's intrigues around the family estate pales in comparison to the devastating consequences that Heathcliff's obsession with revenge brings to everyone around him. *The Impudent Ones* never rises to the tragic dimension that *Wuthering Heights* achieves in the end.

While Emily Brontë was defying the literary strictures of her time, Marguerite Duras had more conventional ambitions with her first novel. Looking back on the days she spent in the Lot-et-Garonne as a child, she seems to have hesitated between a rustic *roman champêtre* and a classic *roman psychologique* in the vein of Paul Bourget. The pastoral component in *The Impudent Ones* follows the naturalistic current of nineteenth-century writers such as George Sand (*The Devil's Pool, The Country Waif*), Emile Zola (*La terre*), or the lesser-known but immensely popular René Bazin, whose novels *La terre qui meurt* (*The Dying Earth*) and *Le blé qui lève* (*The Coming Harvest*) were still must-reads for generations of French high school students. In *The Impudent Ones*, the sections concerning the trees, meadows, fields, and rivers surrounding the family estate of Uderan bear a striking resemblance to similar descriptions of the countryside found in Bazin's hymns to nature. The careful attention paid to class structure in *The Impudent Ones* owes a debt to the theories of André Thérive, one of the three gentlemen whose approval of her manuscript Marguerite Donnadieu put forth in her letter to Gallimard. Thérive, a critic for *Le Temps*, was co-founder of the *École populiste*, a literary movement advocating a return to class portraiture and the study of sociological issues. As evidenced by her novel, the class-conscious author of *The Impudent Ones* was ready to follow Thérive's precepts.

A Manuscript in Search of a Publisher

Arland's reader's report indicates that the manuscript of *La famille Taneran* was given to him by Gallimard at the beginning of March 1941. The author's request for a quick decision was not obliged, however, as Gaston Gallimard was still reeling from attempts by the occupying authorities to take control of his company. That same month, Marguerite Donnadieu's father-in-law died of a heart attack, prompting her mother-in-law to leave occupied Paris and join relatives in Corsica, then still in the "Free Zone." Her daughter-in-law may have planned to accompany her on the trip to the island, as her letter to Gallimard, dated March 31, would suggest:

Sir,

About a month-and-a-half ago, I sent you the manuscript of a novel with the working title La famille Taneran *or* Maud. *I am still in the dark not knowing what you thought of it. I would be most obliged if you would let me know what you have decided, as*

I will probably leave Paris for a while and would like very much
to be informed of your decision before I go. I apologize for rushing
you in this way.

Faithfully Yours,
Marguerite Donnadieu-Antelme[9]

When the author did not receive a reply, she turned to the ever-obliging Pierre Lafue, who agreed to write a letter of support, which he sent on May 8. Opining that any short-comings in the composition of the novel were mere "youthful flaws," easily corrected, he argued: "One could not expect Madame Donnadieu to have already achieved the full mastery of her art. . . . I believe it would be a pity to deprive oneself of a book revealing rather rare qualities."

Gallimard replied to Lafue in a polite letter that the manuscript was not publishable as it was, Madame Donnadieu's writing being "awkward" and "clumsy" in too many places. But he added that *La famille Taneran* was "a very interesting work" nevertheless, which allowed "something" to be expected from its author.[10] On May 16, the writer Raymond Queneau—also a member of Gallimard's reading committee—delivered the verdict directly to Marguerite Duras: "Madame, we have taken a very keen interest in reading your manuscript. It is not possible for us at the moment to undertake its publication, but I would be very happy to be

---

9 Gallimard archives.
10 Gallimard archives.

able to talk to you about it if it were possible for you to call at rue Sébastien-Bottin one of these days."[11]

It would take two more years for the novel to find a publisher. In the spring of 1942, despondent over the loss of her first child (a son who died during childbirth), Marguerite Duras felt the need to look for work. Through her husband's connections, she was hired by a new governmental office established at the request of German authorities, in charge of allotting the diminishing stocks of printing paper (which was a clever way for the occupying forces to exercise full censorship over what could be published or reissued since the lists of books had to be approved by the Propaganda Staffel and the German embassy). After starting as an assistant, "Madame Antelme" shortly became the commission's executive secretary. Although she did not have the power to decide who would be on the lists, her position put her in contact with all the publishing houses still operating in occupied Paris.

Developing a reputation for both her efficiency and her literary inclinations, she was able to recommend friends and acquaintances for the paid task of reviewing manuscripts. Her "recruits" included Pierre Lafue; André Thérive; Ramon Fernandez, a brilliant critic and enthusiastic collaborationist; Jacques-Napoléon Faure-Biguet, a writer friend of the Antelmes; and Dionys Mascolo, a colleague of Albert Camus at Gallimard. (Mascolo became her lover and longtime partner, and the father of her son, after she divorced Robert Antelme in 1947.)

After several rejections and significant rewriting, *La famille*

---

11 Gallimard archives.

Taneran was finally accepted by Librairie Plon—the publisher of Paul Bourget, Julien Green, and Robert Brasillach—most likely after the intercession of Faure-Biguet, whose own works were published by Plon.[12] The book appeared in Paris bookstores in August 1943.[13] The title on the cover had been changed to the more enticing *Les impudents*, and the author had adopted the pen name under which she would ultimately become world-famous.

Jean Vallier, New York, September 28, 2020

---

12 We will probably never know how much rewriting Marguerite Duras did, as no manuscript or notes have survived; but Dionys Mascolo remembered that when he met her, she was still busy making improvements.

13 The same year, Simone de Beauvoir's first novel *L'invitée (The Guest)* was published, as well as Sartre's *L'être et le néant (Being and Nothingness)* and Raymond Queneau's *Pierrot mon ami (Pierrot)*. The year before, Albert Camus's *L'étranger* had been published by Gallimard.

Marguerite Duras (1914–1996) is the internationally known author of the novel *The Lover*, as well as *The War*, *The North China Lover*, *Moderato cantabile*, and the screen-plays of *Hiroshima mon amour* and *India Song*, in addition to many other works.

Kelsey L. Haskett has recently retired as professor of French and chair of the Department of World Languages and Cultures at Trinity Western University in Langley, British Columbia.

Jean Vallier is the author of *C'etait Marguerite Duras*, a two-volume biography published in 2006 and 2010 in Paris by Fayard, reissued in a single volume in 2014 by Le Livre de Poche. He lives in New York and Paris.

PUBLISHING IN
THE PUBLIC INTEREST

Thank you for reading this book published by The New Press. The New Press is a nonprofit, public interest publisher. New Press books and authors play a crucial role in sparking conversations about the key political and social issues of our day.

We hope you enjoyed this book and that you will stay in touch with The New Press. Here are a few ways to stay up to date with our books, events, and the issues we cover:

- Sign up at www.thenewpress.com/subscribe to receive updates on New Press authors and issues and to be notified about local events
- Like us on Facebook: www.facebook.com /newpressbooks
- Follow us on Twitter: www.twitter.com /thenewpress
- Follow us on Instagram: www.instagram.com /thenewpress

Please consider buying New Press books for yourself; for friends and family; or to donate to schools, libraries, community centers, prison libraries, and other organizations involved with the issues our authors write about.

The New Press is a 501(c)(3) nonprofit organization. You can also support our work with a tax-deductible gift by visiting www.thenewpress.com/donate.